# THE WEAVE

*Threads of Choices and Connections*

## DEEPAK SHARMA

"What appears as coincidence is often the work of unseen threads, weaving quietly to shape a life's design."

-   Deepak Sharma

# Disclaimer

This book is a work of fiction. Names, characters, places, events, and incidents are either the product of the author's imagination or used in a fictitious manner. Any resemblance to actual persons, living or dead, or actual events is purely coincidental.

The themes and scenarios explored within this story are meant to provoke thought, inspire reflection, and entertain. While the book draws inspiration from cultural elements, traditions, and universal truths, it does not claim to be an accurate representation of any specific belief system, philosophy, or historical event.

Readers are encouraged to interpret the narrative through their own experiences and perspectives. The author does not intend for the story to serve as advice or a definitive guide on any subject.



Thank you for embracing this story with an open heart and mind.

# Contents

# Preface

Every thread has a story to tell, a purpose to fulfill, and a role to play in the vast tapestry of existence. This book began as a quiet reflection—a personal journey into the interplay of choices, sacrifices, and the unseen connections that shape our lives. What started as a simple idea has evolved into a story that explores the depths of humanity, resilience, and the delicate balance between ambition and identity.

At its core, this is not just a tale of one person's path but an invitation to all readers to look within and reflect on their own journeys. It's about the moments that define us, the threads that bind us to others, and the silent burdens we carry as we navigate an ever-changing world.

Through Aryan's story, I hope to illuminate the universal truths we all share: the search for meaning, the strength it takes to accept vulnerability, and the courage to face the unknown. While this book delves into the fantastical, its heart beats with the rhythm of real, human struggles—those of loss, longing, and redemption.

This book isn't meant to answer every question but to spark new ones. It's meant to leave you thinking about the choices you make, the sacrifices you bear, and the connections you nurture.

As you turn these pages, I hope you find moments that resonate with your own story. May Aryan's journey inspire you to reflect on your own threads and the role you play in the grander weave of life.

Thank you for picking up this book. It's not just Aryan's story—it's yours too.

# Acknowledgment

**W**riting this book has been a journey of discovery, reflection, and immense gratitude. It stands as a testament to the incredible support, encouragement, and inspiration I have received along the way.

First and foremost, I extend my deepest gratitude to my readers. Your curiosity and willingness to embark on this journey with me have been my greatest motivation. This book is as much yours as it is mine.

To my family and close friends, thank you for your unwavering belief in me, even on the days when doubt clouded my vision. Your love and patience have been the foundation upon which this work was built.

To those who have inspired the characters, themes, and lessons within these pages, whether knowingly or unknowingly, you've provided me with the depth and humanity needed to bring this story to life.

I am also deeply thankful for the countless stories, traditions, and cultural roots that have influenced my imagination. They serve as a reminder of the power of storytelling to connect and heal.

Finally, I want to acknowledge everyone who dreams of telling their own story. This book is a small tribute to the courage it takes to give voice to one's thoughts and the belief that every story—every thread—matters. Thank you for being part of this journey.

-    **Deepak Sharma**

# 1

# The Notebook

The rain drummed softly against the windows as Aryan Kapoor stood in the doorway of his father's study. It was the first time he had stepped into the room since the funeral six months ago. The air was heavy with the scent of old paper and varnished wood, mingling with something more elusive memories, perhaps, or guilt.

He told himself this was just another room. Another space in a house too large for one man to inhabit alone. Yet as he crossed the threshold, he couldn't shake the feeling that this study was more alive than any other part of the home.

The desk was cluttered, papers and books spilling across its surface as though Professor Raghuveer Kapoor had simply stepped out for a moment, intending to return to his work. But Aryan knew better. His father wasn't coming back.

Aryan moved closer, his eyes skimming the chaotic desk. Drafts of essays, printouts marked with red ink, an open book with a pen resting between its pages. The room felt frozen in time, a snapshot of a life that revolved around history and stories—stories Aryan had never cared to understand.

His gaze landed on a notebook, set apart from the rest. The leather cover was dark, worn smooth at the edges, with a strange golden emblem pressed into its surface. It wasn't like his father to leave something like this untouched. Raghuveer Kapoor was a man of method, a scholar who prized order. This book, almost reverently placed, demanded attention.

Aryan hesitated before reaching for it. His fingers brushed the leather, and he felt a faint shiver run through him. He opened it to the first page.

The handwriting was unmistakable: strong, deliberate strokes that he recognized from a lifetime of birthday cards, notes, and grocery lists. But the words here weren't ordinary. They were fragments—half-told stories, unfinished thoughts, and musings that stopped mid-sentence. The pages felt chaotic, a far cry from his father's usual precision.

Then his eyes fell on a single line, written in bold letters at the centre of an otherwise empty page:

*"Find the forgotten truths; only then will you understand."*

He read it twice, then a third time. What truths? Forgotten by whom? The words were maddeningly vague, but something about them burrowed under his skin.

Flipping further, he found a map tucked between the pages. It was hand-drawn, its edges smudged and worn. Symbols dotted the landscape—small, intricate icons that marked places he didn't recognize.

Beside each one, his father had scrawled words in a tight, slanted script: *Memory, Echo, Resonance.*

One symbol stood out: a temple, its spire reaching upward like an arrow. Aryan's chest tightened as he stared at it. He had seen this temple before. Not in person, but in his father's stories.

*"It's a place where stories go to live,"* his father had said once, years ago, when Aryan was still young enough to listen. *"And where forgotten stories wait to be found again."*

At the time, Aryan had dismissed it as one of his father's eccentricities, no different from the endless tales about mythical cities and gods who walked among mortals. But now, looking at the map, the words came back to him with startling clarity.

He leaned back in the chair, the notebook resting on his lap. The rain outside had grown heavier, the rhythmic tapping on the glass filling the silence. For years, he had distanced himself from his father's world. Raghuveer Kapoor had lived with his head in the clouds, chasing myths and legends, while Aryan had chosen a safer path—writing articles that paid the bills and built a reputation, if not a legacy.

But what had that left him with? An empty house. A desk without answers.

His hand brushed the map again, and he felt the pull of it—something unexplainable but undeniable. This wasn't just about his father. It was about him, too. About the questions he had been too afraid to ask and the truths he had been too stubborn to see.

The next morning, Aryan packed a small bag. The notebook went in first, tucked securely between layers of clothing. He didn't bother telling anyone he was leaving; there was no one to tell.

Standing in the doorway of the study, he glanced back one last time. The desk, the shelves, the papers—it all felt strangely lighter now, as if the weight of it had shifted.

"I never understood you," he said quietly, his voice barely audible over the rain. "But maybe it's time I tried."

With that, he closed the door and stepped out into the world. The journey ahead was still a mystery, but for the first time in years, Aryan felt alive.

***

# 2

# The Temple's Shadow

The sun hung low on the horizon, casting the world in hues of amber and gold. Aryan adjusted the strap of his backpack as he stepped off the rickety bus that had carried him to the foothills of the Aranya Range. The journey had been long and uncomfortable, but the sight before him—rolling hills dotted with ancient trees—was worth it.

The small town of Karuna lay at the base of the hills, its winding streets alive with the hum of evening activity. Vendors called out to passersby, selling everything from fragrant spices to vibrant fabrics. Children darted between the stalls, their laughter ringing in the warm air.

Aryan paused for a moment, letting the energy of the place seep into him. It was a stark contrast to the sterile silence of his father's study. He tightened his grip on the notebook in his hand, its weight a constant reminder of why he was here.

He had spent the better part of the bus ride poring over its pages, trying to decipher the significance of the map and the symbols it held. The first marked location— labelled "Memory"— seemed to point to a temple nestled deep within the hills.

The Weave - *Threads of Choices and Connections*

A temple where, according to his father's notes, "the stories of the forgotten" were said to reside.

The temple wasn't on any map Aryan could find, and none of the locals he asked seemed to know of its existence. An old woman selling tea had simply smiled when he described it.

"All temples are full of forgotten stories," she had said, pouring steaming chai into a chipped clay cup. "Perhaps it's the stories that find you, not the other way around."

Her words had unsettled him, though he couldn't say why.

The trail to the temple began just beyond the town, marked by an ancient stone archway almost swallowed by vines. Aryan hesitated at the threshold. The path ahead was narrow and steep, disappearing into the dense forest that covered the hills.

He checked his phone—no signal. With a deep breath, he tucked it into his pocket. For all his father's love of legends and myths, Aryan had always been tethered to the practical. And yet, standing there, staring into the shadows of the forest, he couldn't shake the feeling that he was stepping into something far older than himself.

The climb was arduous, the trail winding higher with every step. The air grew cooler as the canopy thickened, and the sounds of the town faded into a hush broken only by the rustle of leaves and the occasional birdcall.

After what felt like hours, the trees parted to reveal a clearing. In the centre stood the temple, its stone facade weathered by time but no less imposing. Intricate carvings covered its surface, depicting scenes of gods and mortals intertwined, their faces worn smooth by centuries of wind and rain.

Aryan approached slowly, his heart pounding in his chest. The temple's doors were ajar, revealing a dark interior. He hesitated at the threshold, a sense of unease prickling at the edges of his mind.

And then he saw it: a faint light flickering deep within the temple, as if beckoning him forward.

The interior was colder than he had expected, the air thick with the scent of damp stone and ancient wood. Aryan's footsteps echoed as he stepped into the main chamber, where the light he had seen came from an oil lamp burning in a small alcove.

Before the lamp stood a statue—a figure he didn't recognize. It wasn't one of the familiar gods he had seen in temples as a child. This figure was cloaked, its face obscured, and its hands outstretched as if offering something unseen.

Beneath the statue lay an inscription, carved into the stone in a script Aryan couldn't read. But the notebook in his bag stirred a memory. Flipping to a page his father had marked; he found a similar script.

"*Smarana*," he whispered, tracing the word with his finger. Memory.

As he spoke, a gust of wind swept through the temple, extinguishing the lamp. Aryan froze, his breath catching in his throat. The room was plunged into darkness, save for a faint glow emanating from the statue itself.

And then, a voice. Low, melodic, and ancient, it filled the chamber, though Aryan couldn't tell where it was coming from.

*"You seek forgotten truths. But are you prepared to bear their weight?"*

The question hung in the air, and Aryan felt an odd pull at his chest. He opened his mouth to respond, but no sound came out.

The glow from the statue grew brighter, illuminating the walls of the chamber. Aryan's eyes widened as he took in the carvings that surrounded him. They were stories—scenes of people standing at crossroads, of battles fought and lost, of choices that changed the course of lives.

And in the centre of it all, a single figure, cloaked and faceless, appearing in each scene like a silent witness.

Aryan stepped closer, his hand trembling as he reached out to touch the carvings. The moment his fingers brushed the stone, a flood of images overwhelmed him—memories that weren't his own, voices that weren't his, all rushing through him in a torrent.

He stumbled back, gasping for air. The statue's glow dimmed, and the temple fell silent once more.

Whatever this place was, it was no ordinary temple. And whatever truths it held, they weren't going to reveal themselves easily.

***

# 3

# The Stranger's Path

The descent back to the town was quicker than Aryan had anticipated, but it left him more disoriented than the climb had. His mind churned with questions as he retraced the narrow path through the forest. The voice, the glow of the statue, the rush of foreign memories—they had all felt too vivid, too real to dismiss as imagination.

By the time he stepped through the stone archway and into Karuna, the town was quieter. Most of the market stalls had closed, leaving the streets bathed in the warm glow of scattered lanterns. He walked without direction, his feet carrying him toward the town square, where an ancient banyan tree spread its roots across the cracked earth.

"Long climb, isn't it?"

The voice startled Aryan, and he turned to see a man sitting on one of the low stone benches that circled the tree. He was older, perhaps in his sixties, with a weathered face and a beard streaked with gray. His clothes were simple, but his eyes held a sharpness that belied his otherwise unassuming appearance.

Aryan hesitated before nodding. "You've been to the temple?"

The man chuckled softly. "I've been everywhere in these hills, my friend. The temple is only the beginning."

There was something in his tone that caught Aryan off guard—an undercurrent of knowing, as though the man had been expecting him.

"I don't think I caught your name," Aryan said cautiously.

"I didn't offer it," the man replied with a small smile. "But you can call me Anant. And you—you're Raghuveer Kapoor's son, aren't you?"

Aryan froze. "How do you know that?"

Anant leaned back against the bench, crossing his arms. "Your father and I crossed paths many years ago. He came here looking for the same thing you are now."

Aryan frowned. "And what is that, exactly?"

Anant's smile faded, and for a moment, his expression was unreadable. "That depends on what you believe you're looking for. Truth? Closure? A purpose greater than yourself?" He gestured to the notebook in Aryan's hand. "Or perhaps just a way to feel close to him again."

The words hit harder than Aryan had expected. He tightened his grip on the notebook, unsure whether to feel angry or exposed.

Anant's gaze softened. "You don't have to answer now. But if you're serious about this journey, you'll need to understand something your father struggled with."

"And what's that?"

"That the truths you seek will ask more of you than you're prepared to give."

The next morning, Aryan awoke to a sharp knock on the door of the small inn where he had rented a room. When he opened it, he found Anant standing there, holding a steaming cup of tea in one hand and a folded piece of paper in the other.

"I figured you might need some direction," Anant said, handing him the paper.

Aryan unfolded it to reveal a sketch—a rough map of the region, with a new location marked in red.

"This," Anant said, tapping the mark, "is where your father's journey faltered. It's a shrine, hidden deep within the eastern forest. The locals call it the Shrine of Echoes."

Aryan raised an eyebrow. "And you expect me to just trust you?"

Anant shrugged. "You trusted the map in that notebook, didn't you? This isn't much different."

There was a logic to his words that Aryan couldn't deny. But there was also something unsettling about Anant's certainty, as though he knew more than he was letting on.

"What's at the shrine?" Aryan asked.

Anant's expression grew serious. "Answers, perhaps. Or more questions. That depends on what you're ready to hear."

The path to the Shrine of Echoes was less defined than the one to the temple had been. Aryan found himself weaving through dense undergrowth, his progress slowed by the tangled roots and low-hanging branches that clawed at his clothes. The air was cooler here, the forest darker, as though the sun had decided it didn't belong in this part of the world.

After hours of trekking, he emerged into a small clearing. The shrine stood at its center, a modest structure of stone and wood, its edges softened by moss and creeping vines. It was unremarkable compared to the grandeur of the temple, but something about it felt... alive.

Aryan stepped closer; his eyes drawn to the carvings that adorned its surface. Unlike the temple, these were simpler, more abstract — patterns of concentric circles and spirals that seemed to pulse faintly in the fading light.

The door to the shrine creaked open as he approached, revealing a dim interior lit by a single beam of sunlight that filtered through a crack in the roof. At the center of the room stood a pedestal, and on it, a small stone tablet engraved with more of the strange script he had seen at the temple.

As Aryan reached out to touch the tablet, a voice echoed through the chamber—not as a sound, but as a presence that filled his mind.

*"Speak your truth, and the echoes will guide you."*

His hand hovered over the tablet, his pulse racing. Speak the truth? What did that even mean?

"I don't know what I'm looking for," he said aloud, his voice trembling. "I don't even know why I'm here."

The chamber grew silent, the air heavy with expectation. And then, the beam of sunlight shifted, illuminating a single word carved into the pedestal beneath the tablet.

*"Seek."*

***

# 4

# Shadows of the Map

Aryan ran his fingers over the worn edges of the map spread across the wooden table. Each symbol on the parchment felt alive, humming with an energy he couldn't yet comprehend. The dimly lit room smelled of old paper and ink, mixed with the faint scent of the forest outside. Kabir watched him from the corner, his face unreadable.

"This map," Aryan said finally, "it's a piece of a puzzle, isn't it? My father left it for me, but why?"

Kabir stepped closer; his movements deliberate. "It's not just a puzzle—it's a key. But every key needs a door, and not all doors lead to answers."

Aryan sighed, leaning back. "You keep speaking in riddles. If you know something, just tell me."

Kabir's sharp eyes softened for a moment. "The truth, Aryan, is never handed to us. Your father didn't leave you instructions because he believed you'd find the answers in your own way. This map—" he tapped its centre, where a symbol resembling the temple's spire was drawn — "is where his search began. And perhaps, where yours must continue."

Aryan stared at the symbol, frustration bubbling beneath his calm exterior. "And what happens when I find whatever this leads to? Do I end up like him? Lost in questions and shadows?"

Kabir didn't answer immediately. Instead, he walked to a shelf and pulled out a small leather-bound journal. He held it out to Aryan. "Your father's words might help you decide. Read this tonight. And tomorrow, we go to the caves."

Aryan hesitated before taking the journal. The leather felt cold against his skin, the cover embossed with a familiar pattern—a tree with roots that extended like veins.

That night, Aryan sat by the small window in his rented room. The journal lay open on his lap, its pages filled with his father's looping handwriting.

*"To search is to embrace the unknown. To understand is to let go of certainty."*

The words struck Aryan like a blow. His father had always been a man of conviction, or so he'd thought. Yet here was a confession of doubt, a vulnerability Aryan had never seen.

The entries were fragmented, each one hinting at discoveries and fears.

*"The temple holds a secret older than the hills. But it isn't the temple itself—it's the path it guards. The map leads beyond the temple, into the mountains. To a place the locals call the Whispering Caves."*

Aryan's fingers tightened around the journal. Whispering Caves? He'd heard tales of them as a child, stories of echoes that carried the voices of the past.

*"I've stood at the mouth of the caves, and I've felt their pull. But I wasn't ready to enter. Not yet. Perhaps someday, Aryan will find the courage I couldn't."*

The last sentence felt like a weight on Aryan's chest. His father had left a path, but also a burden—a legacy intertwined with expectation.

The next morning, Aryan met Kabir at the edge of town. The older man was already prepared, a small satchel slung over his shoulder.

"Ready?" Kabir asked, his tone lighter than Aryan expected.

"No," Aryan admitted, "but I'm going anyway."

Kabir's lips quirked into a faint smile. "That's the spirit."

They walked in silence for most of the journey, the path winding through dense forests and rocky terrain. The air grew colder as they climbed, the sunlight filtered through the canopy above.

As they neared the caves, Aryan felt a strange unease settle over him. The entrance loomed ahead—a dark maw in the mountainside, framed by jagged rocks and overgrown vines.

Kabir stopped just short of the entrance. "This is as far as I go."

Aryan turned to him, surprised. "You're not coming in?"

"The caves are your journey," Kabir said simply. "I'm just a guide."

Aryan stared at the darkness ahead, his pulse quickening. The stories of the Whispering Caves came rushing back—the echoes, the illusions, the dangers. But beneath the fear was a spark of something else: curiosity.

Taking a deep breath, he stepped forward.

The first thing he noticed was the sound. It wasn't silence, but a low hum that seemed to come from the walls themselves. As he moved deeper, the light from the entrance faded, replaced by a faint, otherworldly glow emanating from the rocks.

And then he heard it.

A voice, soft and distant, yet unmistakable.

"Aryan."

He froze, his heart hammering in his chest. The voice was his father's.

"Aryan," it repeated, clearer this time. "You've come."

Tears sprang to Aryan's eyes as he whispered, "Dad?"

But there was no answer, only the hum of the caves growing louder, pulling him further in.

***

# 5

# Echoes of the Depths

The light from the entrance of the caves vanished as Aryan moved deeper, swallowed by the pulsating glow of the crystalline walls. Every step echoed, the sound ricocheting off unseen crevices, creating an eerie symphony. The temperature dropped, and the air turned heavy, carrying the faint metallic tang of earth and time.

The voice that had called him earlier was silent now, but its resonance lingered in Aryan's chest, as if it had planted a seed of memory or expectation.

He gripped the map tightly in his hand, the parchment warm despite the cold. His father's notes had described the caves as both a passage and a labyrinth—a place where the past whispered its secrets to those willing to listen. Aryan wasn't sure if he was ready, but he didn't have the luxury of doubt anymore.

After what felt like hours of navigating narrow passages, Aryan stumbled into a vast chamber. The ceiling arched high above him, encrusted with glowing mineral veins that cast a pale, flickering light. In the centre of the room stood a pedestal of jagged stone, and atop it lay an object shrouded in fabric.

His heart raced as he approached. The pedestal seemed alive, humming faintly with energy that thrummed under his fingertips when he touched it. He hesitated, staring at the covered object. Was this another fragment of his father's trail, or something far older?

Carefully, he pulled back the fabric. Beneath it lay an artefact unlike anything he'd ever seen—a disk of polished obsidian, etched with the same symbols as those on the map. Around its edges, carvings depicted scenes of a civilisation long lost: temples, forests, rivers, and stars.

But what caught Aryan's breath was the image in the centre of the disk—a tree, its branches reaching skyward and its roots twisting deep into the earth. The same symbol embossed on his father's journal.

"Raghuveer Kapoor," a voice said behind him, low and steady.

Aryan whirled around; the disk clutched to his chest.

The figure that stood in the chamber's entrance was cloaked in shadow, but as it stepped forward, the dim light revealed an elderly woman. Her eyes, sharp and piercing, were framed by a face lined with years of wisdom and weariness. She carried a staff that seemed more ceremonial than functional, its top adorned with an intricate carving of the same tree.

"You knew my father?" Aryan asked, his voice shaking.

The woman inclined her head. "I knew him, yes. And I know why you're here."

Aryan narrowed his eyes. "Then tell me. What does this mean?" He held up the disk. "What was he looking for? Why did he leave all of this behind?"

The woman's gaze softened, but her tone remained firm. "Your father was searching for a truth buried deeper than these caves. A truth about our world, and about himself. But what he found was more than he could bear."

Aryan felt a flicker of anger. "And so, he left me to deal with it?"

"No," she said, stepping closer. "He left you a choice."

The woman's name was Devika, and as they sat in the glow of the chamber, she began to unravel the story Aryan had been chasing.

"These caves are sacred," she explained. "Not for what they hold, but for what they reveal. They are mirrors, Aryan. They show us what we carry within—our fears, our desires, our truths. Your father came here seeking answers, but he wasn't ready to face what the caves showed him."

Aryan frowned. "What did they show him?"

Devika paused, her expression heavy. "A vision of a world unravelling. A world where humanity had forgotten its roots, its connection to the earth and to each other. He believed the answers lay in the ancient knowledge of our ancestors; knowledge hidden in places like this."

Aryan looked down at the disk in his hands. "And this? What does it do?"

Devika's eyes darkened. "It is a map, but not of places. It charts the pathways of the soul—the choices that lead us closer to our true selves, or further away. Your father believed it could guide humanity back to harmony, but he also feared its power."

Aryan's mind raced. Could this be the legacy his father had spoken of? A way to make sense of the chaos he'd always felt in the world, and within himself.

"But why me?" he asked, his voice barely above a whisper.

"Because you are the key," Devika said simply. "Your father couldn't complete the journey, but you can. The question is: will you?"

As Devika led Aryan back through the caves, her words echoed in his mind. Every step felt heavier, as if the disk itself carried the weight of the choices ahead. When they emerged into the cold light of dawn, Aryan blinked against the brightness, his thoughts a storm of uncertainty.

Kabir was waiting near the entrance, his expression unreadable as he watched Aryan approach.

"Well?" Kabir asked.

Aryan didn't answer immediately. He held up the disk, its surface gleaming in the morning sun. "What did my father see in this?" Kabir's gaze lingered on the artifact before meeting Aryan's eyes. "Not what he saw," he said quietly.

"What he couldn't unsee." Aryan's grip on the disk tightened. Whatever lay ahead, he knew there was no turning back now.

***

# 6

# The Fork in the Path

The climb back to the village was quiet, the weight of the disk hanging heavy in Aryan's satchel. Each step felt like a question he didn't know how to answer. Devika's words circled in his mind — *"It charts the pathways of the soul."* What did that even mean? And why had his father chosen to keep it from him?

Kabir walked a few paces ahead, his posture unusually rigid. The silence between them felt strained, and Aryan couldn't shake the feeling that Kabir knew more than he was letting on.

Finally, Aryan broke the quiet. "You've seen this disk before, haven't you?"

Kabir stopped mid-step, turning slowly. His expression was unreadable, but his eyes betrayed a flicker of something—guilt, perhaps, or fear. "I've seen many things, Aryan. Some better left unseen."

"That's not an answer."

Kabir sighed, running a hand through his greying hair. "Your father trusted me to protect you, not to burden you with truths you might not be ready for."

Aryan's temper flared. "Protect me? From what? From understanding my own life? My father's life?" He stepped closer, his voice rising. "You don't get to decide what I'm ready for, Kabir. That's my choice."

For a moment, Kabir looked as if he might argue, but then his shoulders sagged. "You're right," he said softly. "You deserve to know."

They stopped in a clearing near the edge of the forest, the sun casting long shadows through the trees. Kabir sat on a fallen log, motioning for Aryan to join him.

"Your father and I weren't just friends," Kabir began. "We were partners—explorers of sorts. He had a way of seeing the world, of finding meaning in places others overlooked. It wasn't just wanderlust; it was a calling. And that calling led him here, to this village, to those caves."

Aryan listened intently, his earlier anger fading into curiosity.

"He believed the disk was part of something much bigger," Kabir continued. "A relic from an ancient civilisation that understood the world in ways we've forgotten. They saw life as a delicate balance—between humans and nature, between progress and preservation. Your father thought the disk held the key to restoring that balance."

"But?" Aryan prompted, sensing the hesitation in Kabir's voice.

"But the closer he got to the truth, the more it consumed him," Kabir admitted. "He started seeing enemies everywhere—

people who would exploit the disk's power, twist it for their own gain. He didn't trust anyone. Not even me."

Aryan stared at the ground, his thoughts swirling. He wanted to be angry at his father for abandoning him, for leaving behind so many unanswered questions. But he also felt a pang of empathy. The search for something so profound—it must have been lonely.

"What happened to him?" Aryan asked quietly.

Kabir's gaze grew distant. "One day, he went back to the caves. He said he needed to face the truth, to understand what the disk was asking of him. He never came out."

The words hit Aryan like a punch to the chest. He'd always imagined his father had left him willingly, choosing his quest over his family. But now, the reality seemed far more complicated—and far more tragic.

By the time they reached the village, the sky had darkened, a storm brewing on the horizon. Aryan's mind was a storm of its own, filled with conflicting emotions and unanswered questions.

He returned to his room and placed the disk on the table, staring at it as if it might suddenly reveal its secrets. The tree etched into its surface seemed to glow faintly in the dim light, its branches and roots intertwining like veins.

"Pathways of the soul," Aryan murmured, tracing the carving with his finger. What pathways had his father seen? And what pathways lay ahead for him?

That night, Aryan dreamed of the caves. He was standing in the chamber where he'd found the disk, but it was different—alive. The walls pulsed with light, the symbols shifting and rearranging themselves like a living puzzle.

In the centre of the room stood his father, his back turned.

"Dad?" Aryan called, his voice echoing.

His father turned slowly, his face etched with both sorrow and determination. "The answers aren't in the caves, Aryan," he said, his voice faint but clear. "They're in you."

Aryan woke with a start, his heart pounding. The room was dark, but the disk on the table seemed to glimmer faintly, as if echoing his father's words.

The next morning, Aryan found Kabir waiting outside, his expression serious.

"There's someone you need to meet," Kabir said without preamble.

"Who?" Aryan asked, surprised.

"Someone who might have the answers you're looking for," Kabir replied. "But be warned—they'll ask more of you than you might be ready to give."

Aryan's stomach tightened with a mix of anticipation and dread. He nodded. "Let's go."

As they left the village, Aryan couldn't shake the feeling that he was standing at a crossroads, the choices ahead as uncertain and winding as the paths through the forest. And somewhere deep inside, he knew: the journey was only just beginning.

***

# 7

# The Sage of the Forgotten

The journey from the village took them through landscapes that seemed untouched by time. Towering banyan trees draped in vines framed the winding dirt path, their roots like gnarled sentinels guarding secrets of the earth. Kabir led the way in silence, his steps purposeful but unhurried. Aryan followed, his gaze drifting to the satchel where the disk was safely tucked away. It felt heavier with each mile, as though its significance was growing with every step.

"Where are we going?" Aryan asked finally, breaking the silence.

"To someone who understands things better than either of us," Kabir replied without looking back. "But she's not like Devika. Be prepared for... challenges."

Aryan frowned. He didn't know whether to feel apprehensive or intrigued.

Hours later, they reached the edge of a cliff, where the land seemed to fall away into an endless expanse of forest below. Perched precariously on the edge was a weathered hut, its thatched roof bending under the weight of time. A faint wisp of smoke curled from the chimney, the only sign of life.

Kabir stopped and turned to Aryan. "She doesn't take kindly to strangers. But if she sees you as worthy, she might help."

"Worthy of what?" Aryan asked.

Kabir gave him a cryptic smile. "That's for her to decide."

They approached the hut, and Kabir rapped sharply on the wooden door.

"Who disturbs the quiet?" came a voice from within—sharp, commanding, yet strangely melodic.

"It's Kabir," he replied. "And someone you should meet."

There was a long pause, then the sound of a latch clicking. The door creaked open, revealing a woman who seemed as old as the mountains themselves. Her hair was a cascade of silver, her skin lined with the maps of countless years. But her eyes—her eyes were a piercing green, alight with an intelligence that seemed to see straight through Aryan.

"So, this is the boy," she said, her voice softer now, but still laced with authority.

Aryan bristled at the word *boy* but held his tongue.

The woman stepped aside, motioning them in. "Come. The storm is close."

The inside of the hut was dimly lit, with shelves crammed full of jars, scrolls, and objects Aryan couldn't begin to identify. A faint aroma of herbs and earth filled the air. The woman moved with surprising agility for her age, setting a kettle on the fire and gesturing for them to sit.

"I am Ira," she said simply. "And you, I assume, are Aryan."

He nodded.

"I know why you're here," Ira continued, her gaze flicking briefly to the satchel at his side. "That artifact you carry—it is not just an object. It is a question. And every question demands an answer."

Aryan felt his throat tighten. "What kind of answer?"

Ira smiled faintly. "That depends on you. The disk is a mirror—it reflects the truths you carry, the choices you've made and have yet to make. But it also holds the potential for great harm, should it fall into the wrong hands."

Aryan leaned forward. "Then why did my father search for it? Why leave it to me?"

Ira's expression turned grave. "Because he believed you could finish what he started. He saw in you the strength to face the truths he could not."

Kabir spoke for the first time since entering the hut. "Ira, tell him about the Veil."

Aryan glanced between them. "The Veil?"

"It's what your father was trying to uncover," Ira explained. "A barrier—not physical, but spiritual. It separates the world as we know it from a deeper reality. The disk is one of the keys to understanding it, to piercing the Veil and seeing what lies beyond."

Aryan shook his head. "This sounds like something out of a fantasy. How can I be expected to believe any of this?"

Ira fixed him with a steely gaze. "Belief is irrelevant. The Veil exists whether you acknowledge it or not. The question is whether you have the courage to step through it."

Ira rose and retrieved a small wooden box from a shelf. She placed it in front of Aryan, her hands lingering on its surface. "Your father left this with me before he disappeared. He said you would know when it was time to open it."

Aryan's heart pounded as he reached for the box. The wood was smooth and warm, etched with the same tree symbol as the disk. He hesitated, then lifted the lid.

Inside was a folded piece of parchment and a small stone, smooth and black, with faint carvings that glowed faintly in the dim light. Aryan unfolded the parchment and saw his father's handwriting:

*"Aryan, the path will test you. It will demand everything, but it will also give you the clarity you've always sought. Trust yourself. And when you doubt, remember the roots of the tree are as vital as its branches."*

Ira watched him closely. "The stone is a guide," she said. "It will react to the disk and help you navigate the choices ahead. But it cannot choose for you."

Aryan clenched the note in his hand, his father's words cutting through the haze of doubt. "What happens if I fail?"

"The world as we know it continues," Ira said simply. "But the balance your father sought—the harmony between humanity and the greater truth—will remain lost. And with it, the chance for something extraordinary."

As they left the hut, the storm finally broke, rain pouring in torrents. Aryan clutched the box and the disk tightly, the weight of his father's legacy pressing heavier than ever. Kabir walked beside him in silence, the sound of rain and thunder their only companions.

Finally, Aryan spoke. "Do you think he believed I could really do this?"

Kabir glanced at him, a rare softness in his expression. "I think he hoped you'd find your own reason to try."

Aryan nodded, his resolve hardening. Whatever lay ahead, he knew one thing for certain: he couldn't turn back now.

***

# 8

# Shadows in the Light

The rain continued unabated, each drop striking like a drumbeat on the canopy above. Aryan and Kabir moved cautiously through the dense forest, the mud sucking at their boots and the air heavy with the scent of wet earth. The stone Ira had given Aryan hung around his neck now, glowing faintly with every step.

"What's it reacting to?" Aryan asked, his voice low.

Kabir scanned the horizon, his expression unreadable. "It's not just the stone. It's you. The disk and the stone are amplifiers—tools that respond to your intentions and fears alike. You must be deliberate with your thoughts, Aryan. The path ahead is as much about clarity as courage."

Aryan didn't respond. He gripped the satchel tightly, its contents a constant reminder of his father's faith in him. Faith he wasn't sure he deserved.

Hours passed, and the forest began to change. The air grew colder, the trees taller and more imposing, their branches entwined to form a near-impenetrable ceiling. Strange markings appeared on the trunks—symbols that seemed to pulse with a life of their own.

Kabir stopped suddenly, holding up a hand.

"What is it?" Aryan whispered, his heart racing.

Kabir didn't answer. Instead, he knelt and pressed his palm to the ground, closing his eyes. Aryan watched as Kabir's breathing slowed, his body unnaturally still. Then, without warning, Kabir's eyes snapped open.

"We're not alone."

Aryan felt a chill run down his spine. "Who—what is it?"

Kabir stood, his hand resting on the hilt of the dagger at his side. "Not all who seek the Veil do so for enlightenment. Some are drawn to its power, its secrets. And they'll stop at nothing to claim what you carry."

Aryan's grip on the satchel tightened. "Are you saying they're after me?"

"They're after what you have," Kabir corrected. "But yes, that makes you, their target."

Before Aryan could respond, a low, guttural sound echoed through the forest. It wasn't an animal's cry—it was something else, something unnatural.

Kabir moved quickly, pulling Aryan behind a thick tree trunk. "Stay here. Don't make a sound."

"What are you going to do?" Aryan hissed.

"Buy you time."

Kabir disappeared into the shadows, his movements as silent as the falling rain. Aryan pressed his back against the tree, his heart pounding in his chest. He clutched the stone around his neck, willing it to stop glowing, to stop giving away their position.

The sound grew louder, closer. Aryan could make out shapes moving through the underbrush—tall, humanoid figures with elongated limbs and glowing eyes. They moved with a predatory grace, their heads turning sharply as though sniffing the air.

Aryan's mind raced. What were they? And how had his journey led to this moment—hiding from creatures that felt like they belonged to another world entirely?

A sudden burst of light shattered the darkness. Kabir had reappeared, wielding the dagger now alight with a brilliant blue glow. He moved with a fluidity that Aryan could only describe as otherworldly, each strike precise and deliberate. The creatures shrieked and recoiled, their forms flickering like shadows in the light.

"Run!" Kabir shouted, his voice cutting through the chaos.

Aryan didn't need to be told twice. He bolted through the forest, branches clawing at his face and arms. The stone around his neck seemed to pulse in rhythm with his frantic heartbeat, guiding his steps even as his mind screamed at him to stop, to hide.

He stumbled into a clearing and fell to his knees, gasping for air. The satchel had come loose in the chaos, its contents spilling onto the ground. The disk lay in the dirt, its surface shimmering with an unearthly light.

Aryan reached for it but froze as a figure stepped into the clearing.

It wasn't one of the creatures. This was a man, tall and imposing, his face obscured by a hood. He carried no weapon, but his presence was enough to make Aryan's blood run cold.

"You have no idea what you're holding, do you?" the man said, his voice low and menacing.

Aryan scrambled to his feet, clutching the disk to his chest. "Who are you?"

The man tilted his head, as though considering the question. "A seeker, like you. But unlike you, I understand the power of what you carry. Hand it over, and I'll spare you the pain of learning it the hard way."

Aryan shook his head, taking a step back. "This isn't yours to take."

The man laughed, a sound devoid of humour. "You think it's yours? That's cute. But let me make this simple—either you give it to me, or I take it from your lifeless hands."

Before Aryan could respond, the stone around his neck flared to life, its glow so intense that it illuminated the entire clearing. The man recoiled, shielding his eyes.

The Weave - *Threads of Choices and Connections*

In that moment, Aryan felt something shift within him—a surge of resolve, of power he didn't fully understand but knew he couldn't ignore.

"No," he said, his voice steady. "You can't have it."

The man lowered his hand, his eyes narrowing. "So be it."

The air between them seemed to crackle with energy, a tension that Aryan could feel in his very bones. He didn't know what was about to happen, but he knew one thing for certain: this was only the beginning.

***

# 9

# Threads of Destiny

The forest was alive with tension, its once-familiar embrace now a maze of shadows and echoes. Aryan ran, the disk clutched tightly in his arms, the hooded man's chilling words ringing in his ears.

"You can't escape what you're meant to face."

Kabir had always told him that courage was born in the moments you wanted to flee the most. But Aryan felt no courage now—only fear and a strange pull from the artifact in his hands. The disk felt warm against his skin, almost as if it were urging him to move faster, to trust it.

"Where are you leading me?" he whispered, though he knew the disk wouldn't answer.

Behind him, the forest erupted in chaos. Branches snapped, and the guttural cries of the creatures returned, more frenzied this time. Aryan didn't dare look back. He plunged deeper into the woods, his legs aching with every step.

Minutes—or perhaps hours—passed before he stumbled onto a clearing, lit by the soft glow of moonlight filtering through the canopy. In the centre stood a structure unlike anything Aryan had ever seen.

It was a monolith, ancient and weathered, its surface covered in carvings that seemed to move when he wasn't looking directly at them. Symbols swirled and danced, forming patterns that made Aryan's head spin.

The disk in his hands grew warmer, vibrating slightly. Aryan took a hesitant step forward, drawn to the monolith despite the unease coiling in his chest.

As he approached, the carvings seemed to respond to his presence, glowing faintly. The symbols on the monolith mirrored those etched onto the disk, as if they were pieces of the same puzzle.

"This has to mean something," Aryan murmured, his voice barely audible.

He reached out to touch the surface but stopped short when he heard footsteps behind him.

"Don't," Kabir's voice cut through the silence.

Aryan turned to see Kabir emerge from the shadows, his face pale and strained. He held his dagger loosely, its glow dim but steady.

"Kabir! You're alive!" Relief flooded Aryan's voice.

"For now," Kabir said, his tone grim. "But touching that monolith without understanding its purpose could destroy everything—including you."

Aryan frowned, looking back at the monolith. "It's reacting to the disk. It feels like it's guiding me here. Isn't that what we were looking for?"

Kabir shook his head. "The artifact isn't a guide. It's a key. And keys only unlock doors—they don't tell you what's on the other side."

The weight of Kabir's words settled heavily on Aryan. "Then what do we do? We can't keep running forever."

"No," Kabir agreed. "But we also can't act blindly. This place, this monolith—it's a marker, a waypoint on your journey. It's meant to test you, not provide answers."

Aryan's frustration boiled over. "Test me how? By sending monsters after me? By dragging me into something I never asked for?"

Kabir's gaze softened. "Your father chose you, Aryan. Not because you were ready, but because he believed you could become ready. This journey isn't just about the artifact—it's about you."

Before Aryan could respond, a low hum filled the air. The monolith began to glow brighter, its symbols pulsing in time with the vibrations of the disk.

Kabir's eyes widened. "It's reacting to your emotions. Whatever you're feeling, it's amplifying."

Aryan stepped back, panic rising in his chest. The carvings on the monolith grew more erratic, their movements chaotic. The ground beneath their feet trembled, and a sharp crack split the air as a fissure opened in the earth nearby.

"Aryan, calm down!" Kabir shouted.

"I'm trying!" Aryan yelled back, but his mind was a storm of fear, doubt, and frustration. The artifact felt like a living thing now, its energy coursing through him, overwhelming his senses.

Kabir moved quickly, grabbing Aryan by the shoulders. "Listen to me! Focus on one thing—something that grounds you. Your father, the village, anything! Find your centre, or this place will tear itself apart."

Aryan closed his eyes, struggling to steady his breathing. Images flashed through his mind—his father's warm smile, the quiet mornings in the village, the laughter of children playing by the river.

Slowly, the storm within him began to subside. The monolith's glow steadied, its symbols falling into a gentle rhythm once more. The fissure in the ground sealed itself, leaving only silence in its wake.

Kabir released him, his expression a mix of relief and exhaustion. "That was close."

Aryan looked at the monolith, his chest heaving. "It... it responds to me."

Kabir nodded. "And now you know why you need to control your thoughts. The artifact is powerful, but it's also dangerous. You can't let your emotions control it—or you."

Aryan swallowed hard, the weight of his responsibility settling heavily on his shoulders. "What do we do now?"

Kabir glanced at the monolith; his brow furrowed. "We move forward. But first, you need to understand what you're up against."

He gestured for Aryan to sit, pulling a small, weathered scroll from his satchel. Unfurling it, he revealed a map, its surface marked with symbols similar to those on the monolith.

"This journey isn't just about the Veil or the artifact," Kabir said. "It's about the balance between worlds—the one we know, and the one just beyond our reach. The artifact is a bridge, Aryan, but bridges go both ways. If you're not careful, what you let through could destroy everything you're trying to protect."

Aryan stared at the map, the weight of Kabir's words sinking in. He had thought this journey was about uncovering his father's legacy, but now it was clear—it was about so much more.

And he wasn't sure he was ready.

***

# 10

# Echoes of the Unknown

The forest stretched endlessly before them, its silence heavy with secrets. Aryan walked beside Kabir, the weight of the artifact around his neck a constant reminder of the danger they faced. The light from the disk had dimmed, but its faint hum pulsed in rhythm with his heartbeat, a quiet companion to their journey.

"Do you ever wonder why it was you?" Aryan asked, breaking the silence.

Kabir glanced at him; his eyes shadowed by the canopy overhead. "Why what was me?"

"Why my father trusted you to guide me," Aryan clarified. "You seem like someone who works alone. Why take on a burden that wasn't yours to begin with?"

Kabir's lips twitched into a faint smile, though it didn't reach his eyes. "Your father saved my life once. This is my way of repaying a debt I can never truly repay."

Aryan frowned. "Saved your life? How?"

Kabir didn't answer immediately. He reached up to brush a low-hanging branch aside, his movements deliberate. "That's a story for another time. Right now, we need to focus on the path ahead."

The terrain grew rockier as they climbed, the forest giving way to a rugged mountainside. The air was thinner here, sharper, carrying a chill that bit through Aryan's jacket.

"Where are we going?" Aryan asked, struggling to keep up with Kabir's long strides.

"There's a place I know—a sanctuary," Kabir said. "It's hidden, safe. We'll rest there and figure out our next move."

Aryan nodded, though he couldn't shake the feeling that Kabir wasn't telling him everything. The man's past was a puzzle, each piece more cryptic than the last.

As they climbed, the landscape opened up, revealing a breathtaking view of the valley below. Aryan paused, his chest tightening at the sight. The village was a distant speck, almost invisible against the vastness of the world around it.

"It feels so far away," he murmured.

Kabir stopped beside him; his gaze fixed on the horizon. "It is. But distance doesn't erase what's important. It only tests how far you're willing to go to protect it."

Aryan looked at Kabir, surprised by the depth of his words. For a moment, the gruff warrior seemed almost vulnerable.

"Do you miss it?" Aryan asked.

Kabir's expression hardened. "Miss what?"

"Home."

Kabir didn't respond. Instead, he turned and continued up the path, leaving Aryan to wonder what kind of home a man like Kabir could have lost.

They reached the sanctuary just as the sun began to set. It wasn't much—just a small cave hidden behind a curtain of ivy—but it offered shelter from the elements.

Kabir lit a small fire, its warmth a welcome relief from the cold. Aryan sat across from him, the disk resting on his lap.

"What now?" Aryan asked.

Kabir leaned back against the cave wall, his expression thoughtful. "Now, we wait."

"For what?"

"For answers."

Aryan's frustration boiled over. "That's all you ever say — 'wait,' 'be patient.' But I'm tired of waiting. I need to know what's going on, why this artifact is so important, and why I'm the one carrying it."

Kabir studied Aryan for a long moment before speaking. "The artifact isn't just a key. It's a mirror. It reflects what's inside you—your fears, your hopes, your strength. That's why your father chose you, Aryan. Not because you're the strongest or the smartest, but because you have the heart to see this through."

Aryan looked down at the disk, its surface smooth and cool under his fingertips. "But what if I don't? What if I fail?"

Kabir's voice softened. "Failure isn't falling. It's refusing to get back up. As long as you keep moving forward, you haven't failed." The fire crackled, filling the silence between them. Aryan thought about his father, the man who had believed in him even when Aryan hadn't believed in himself.

"Tell me about him," Aryan said quietly.

Kabir raised an eyebrow. "Your father?"

Aryan nodded. "You said he saved your life. How?"

Kabir's gaze drifted to the flames, his expression distant. "It was years ago. I was... lost. Wandering, searching for something I couldn't name. Your father found me, gave me a purpose. He saw something in me that I didn't see in myself."

Aryan leaned forward. "What did he see?"

Kabir's lips quirked into a wry smile. "Someone worth saving."

The weight of Kabir's words settled heavily in Aryan's chest. He thought about the people in his own life—those he had left behind in the village, those he might never see again.

"Do you ever wonder if he made a mistake?" Aryan asked.

Kabir met his gaze, his eyes steady. "Not for a second."

The night deepened, the fire dying down to embers. Aryan lay on the hard ground, the disk tucked safely under his arm. Despite the chill, he felt a strange warmth—a flicker of hope that hadn't been there before.

As sleep claimed him, he dreamed of his father. But this time, the dream wasn't of loss or regret. It was of a man who believed in him, who had entrusted him with a burden not out of obligation, but out of love.

And for the first time, Aryan began to believe in himself, too.

***

# The Veil's Whisper

*Beneath the stars, where shadows play,*

*Lies a path unseen, both night and day.*

*A thread of fate, a tethered spark,*

*Guiding the lost through the vast and dark.*


*What lies beyond the bridge you hold?*

*A treasure vast, or a tale untold?*

*The disk may glow, its secrets deep,*

*But truths it guards aren't yours to keep.*


*Will courage rise when the storm is near?*

*Can you face the void without your fear?*

*Each step ahead, a test unknown,*

*Through worlds unbound, yet not alone.*


*The mirror reflects what lies inside,*

*Your hopes, your doubts, the truths you hide.*

*But beware, young soul, for light and flame,*

*Can heal the world—or curse the same.*

The Weave - *Threads of Choices and Connections*


*What will you choose when the time is near?*

*Will wisdom triumph, or yield to fear?*

*The Veil is thin, the bridge swings wide,*

*But destiny walks by no one's side.*


*So, tread with care, and hold it tight,*

*Your heart, your strength, your inner light.*

*For the key you bear is more than it seems—*

*A gate to ruin, or a world of dreams.*

***

# 11

# The Weight of Words

The firelight flickered, casting jagged shadows on the cave walls. Kabir sat cross-legged; his gaze fixed on the glowing embers. Aryan watched him in silence, his mind replaying the cryptic poem Kabir had recited hours ago. It wasn't just words; it felt like a warning, or perhaps a challenge.

"Why did you tell me that?" Aryan finally asked, breaking the stillness.

Kabir looked up, his eyes sharp but calm. "Because you need to understand what you're carrying. The artifact isn't just a tool—it's a choice. A dangerous one."

Aryan frowned, clutching the disk tightly. "A choice for what? I still don't understand why this thing matters so much."

Kabir leaned forward, the firelight dancing in his eyes. "The Veil separates what we know from what we don't. It's a barrier, protecting this world from what lies beyond. That artifact isn't just a key to open the Veil—it's a question: should it even be opened?"

The words hung in the air like smoke. Aryan felt a chill crawl down his spine.

The next morning, the two ventured further up the mountain, the terrain growing harsher with every step. The wind howled, biting at their faces and whipping Aryan's scarf around his neck. Kabir moved steadily ahead, unbothered by the cold, while Aryan struggled to keep pace.

"Where are we going?" Aryan called over the wind.

"To the shrine," Kabir replied without turning.

"What shrine?"

Kabir stopped abruptly, turning to face Aryan. "A place where your questions might find answers. But answers come at a cost, Aryan. Be sure you're ready to pay it."

Aryan met Kabir's gaze, the man's intensity both unnerving and grounding. "I didn't come this far to turn back now," he said firmly.

Kabir nodded and resumed walking. "Good. Let's hope you mean that."

The shrine was unlike anything Aryan had ever seen. Nestled in the side of the mountain, it was a circular chamber carved from the rock itself. Intricate carvings covered the walls, depicting scenes of battles, sacrifices, and what Aryan could only describe as a great divide—a glowing line splitting the sky and earth.

At the centre of the chamber stood a pedestal, its surface polished to a mirror-like sheen. Kabir approached it cautiously, gesturing for Aryan to follow.

"This is the Echo," Kabir said, his voice reverent. "It reflects the essence of the one who stands before it. A glimpse of who you are—and who you might become."

Aryan hesitated, his gaze shifting between Kabir and the pedestal. "What am I supposed to do?"

"Place the artifact on the Echo," Kabir instructed. "Let it show you what you need to see."

With trembling hands, Aryan placed the artifact on the pedestal. The moment it touched the surface, the chamber seemed to hum with energy. Light rippled across the carvings, illuminating the scenes in a dazzling display.

Aryan stepped back as the light coalesced into a figure—a shadowy silhouette that mirrored his own. The figure moved independently, its eyes glowing like embers.

"Who are you?" Aryan whispered, his voice barely audible.

The silhouette tilted its head, its expression unreadable. "I am you," it said, its voice an echo of Aryan's own. "And I am not."

Aryan's heart pounded in his chest. "What does that mean?"

The figure stepped closer, its presence both familiar and alien. "You carry the weight of many paths, Aryan. Each step you take shapes the world around you. But the artifact... it shapes you. Do you understand the power it holds?"

Aryan shook his head. "No. That's why I'm here. I need to understand."

The figure smiled, a shadow of emotion flickering across its face. "Then ask yourself this: what do you fear most? The power to change the world—or the power to fail it?"

The light faded, and the figure dissolved into smoke, leaving Aryan alone with his thoughts. He turned to Kabir, his voice shaking. "What did I just see?"

Kabir's expression was unreadable. "A reflection. The Echo shows what lies within you—your doubts, your strengths, your fears. It doesn't give answers, Aryan. It only asks questions."

Aryan clenched his fists, frustration boiling over. "But I don't have time for more questions! I need to know what to do!"

Kabir placed a hand on Aryan's shoulder, his grip firm but steady. "The answers will come. But first, you have to face the questions. That's the only way forward."

As they left the shrine, Aryan couldn't shake the image of the shadowy figure—or its haunting words. The artifact felt heavier than ever, its presence a constant reminder of the choice that lay ahead.

But for the first time, Aryan felt something else alongside his fear.

Resolve.

***

# 12

# The Path Divides

The descent from the shrine was harder than the climb. The mountain seemed steeper, the winds harsher. Aryan's steps faltered as his thoughts churned, the Echo's words a drumbeat in his mind. *The power to change the world—or the power to fail it.*

Kabir walked ahead, steady and silent as ever. Aryan envied his calm. "Kabir," he called, his voice barely carrying over the wind. "What if I don't have the answers when it matters?"

Kabir stopped, turning slowly. "No one ever does," he said, his voice quiet but firm. "Answers don't come before the moment—they come *in* it. And when they do, they're shaped by the choices you've made along the way."

Aryan swallowed hard, unsure if Kabir's words comforted him or only deepened his doubts.

They reached a plateau by evening, where a makeshift camp awaited. Kabir moved efficiently, kindling a fire and unpacking supplies. Aryan sat nearby, staring at the artifact in his hands. Its surface shimmered faintly, as if alive.

The Weave - *Threads of Choices and Connections*

"Do you ever wonder," Aryan began, "why *me*? Why was this thing left for *me* and not someone else?"

Kabir paused, glancing at him. "You think it was chance?"

Aryan shrugged. "Maybe. Maybe it was just bad luck."

Kabir shook his head. "The artifact chose you, Aryan. Not because you're special, but because you're capable. There's a difference."

Aryan frowned. "Capable of what?"

"Enduring," Kabir said simply.

As the night deepened, Kabir pulled out a worn journal. Aryan watched as the older man flipped through its pages, his expression softening. "What's that?" Aryan asked.

Kabir held it up. "A record of my failures—and a few of my triumphs."

Aryan raised an eyebrow. "You keep track of those?"

Kabir chuckled. "Not for me. For those who come after. Mistakes are only wasted if no one learns from them."

He handed the journal to Aryan, who hesitated before opening it. The pages were filled with sketches, notes, and fragments of poetry. One line caught Aryan's eye:

*"Courage is not the absence of fear, but the refusal to let it dictate your path."*

Aryan looked up. "Did you write this?"

Kabir nodded. "It's something I've had to remind myself many times."

Aryan's grip on the journal tightened. "Do you ever regret it? Carrying this burden?"

Kabir's eyes darkened. "Regret? No. But it's not without its cost."

The next morning, the landscape changed. The air grew warmer, the snow giving way to rocky terrain. They approached a narrow gorge, its walls steep and unyielding. Kabir paused at the edge, scanning the path ahead.

"This is where we part ways," he said abruptly.

Aryan blinked, taken aback. "What? Why?"

Kabir pointed across the gorge. "The path ahead is yours alone. I've guided you as far as I can."

"But I'm not ready!" Aryan protested.

Kabir placed a hand on Aryan's shoulder. "You are. You just don't know it yet."

Aryan's chest tightened as he looked at the narrow bridge stretching across the gorge. The far side seemed impossibly distant.

"What if I fail?" he whispered.

Kabir's gaze softened. "Then fail. And get up again. That's the only way forward."

The Weave - *Threads of Choices and Connections*

Aryan took a deep breath, stepping onto the bridge. The planks creaked under his weight, the wind tugging at him like unseen hands. He kept his eyes on the far side, refusing to look down.

Halfway across, a sudden gust nearly knocked him off balance. Aryan gripped the ropes, his heart pounding. *One step at a time,* he told himself. *Just one step at a time.*

When he finally reached the other side, he turned back, expecting to see Kabir watching. But the man was gone, the path behind him empty.

Aryan stood there for a long moment, the realization sinking in. From here on, he was truly alone.

The landscape on this side of the gorge was strange, almost otherworldly. The rocks shimmered faintly, as if touched by an unseen light. Aryan felt a strange energy in the air, both comforting and unsettling.

He walked for hours, his thoughts a whirlwind of fear and determination. As the sun began to set, he came across a clearing. At its centre stood a solitary tree, its branches heavy with golden leaves.

Drawn to it, Aryan approached cautiously. Beneath the tree lay a stone tablet, its surface etched with unfamiliar symbols. As he knelt to examine it, the artifact in his hand began to glow.

The symbols on the tablet shifted, rearranging themselves into words he could read:

*"To open the Veil is to see the truth. But truth is not without its price."*

Aryan's breath caught. The tablet's glow faded, leaving him alone beneath the tree.

He sat there for a long time, the weight of the journey pressing down on him. The questions swirled in his mind, unrelenting:

What truth did the Veil hold?  And was he ready to face it?

***

# 13

# Shadows of Truth

The night under the golden tree was restless. Aryan sat with his back against the trunk, the artifact resting in his lap. The glow it once carried had dimmed, as if waiting for something. Around him, the silence of the clearing was absolute—no rustling leaves, no whisper of wind.

His mind churned. The cryptic message on the tablet replayed in his head like an unsolvable riddle. *"To open the Veil is to see the truth. But truth is not without its price."*

"What price?" he muttered to himself. His voice sounded small against the vast quiet.

He traced the edges of the artifact with his fingers, feeling its cool, smooth surface. "Why does everyone talk in riddles?" he said aloud, frustration creeping into his tone.

The artifact pulsed faintly, a soft thrum that resonated in his chest. Aryan froze.

"What was that?"

The pulse came again, stronger this time. The artifact's surface shimmered faintly, its patterns shifting like ripples in water.

Aryan rose to his feet, clutching the artifact tightly. The clearing seemed to darken around him, the golden tree casting elongated shadows. The air grew heavy, pressing against his chest.

And then, a voice—low, resonant, and impossibly close.

*"Do you seek the truth, Aryan?"*

He spun around, heart hammering. "Who's there?"

The shadows at the edge of the clearing stirred, coalescing into a figure. It wasn't like the Echo he'd seen before; this figure was more distinct, its form almost human but not quite. Its eyes glowed like molten gold, unblinking and piercing.

Aryan stepped back, his grip tightening on the artifact. "What are you?"

The figure tilted its head, a faint smile playing on its lips. *"What I am is less important than what you are becoming."*

The figure moved closer, its steps soundless. "You carry the key to the Veil, yet you hesitate. Why?"

Aryan swallowed hard. "Because I don't know what's on the other side. And everyone keeps warning me about the consequences."

The figure's smile widened. "Caution is wise, but fear is a cage. Tell me, Aryan—what do you *hope* to find beyond the Veil?"

Aryan hesitated, the question catching him off guard. "I... I don't know. Answers, maybe. Understanding."

The Weave - *Threads of Choices and Connections*

The figure's golden eyes gleamed. "Answers are dangerous things. They change those who seek them. Are you prepared to be changed?"

The question hung in the air, heavy and unrelenting. Aryan felt a surge of defiance. "I didn't come this far to turn back now," he said firmly.

The figure regarded him for a long moment before nodding. "Very well. But know this: the Veil guards' truths that are both wondrous and terrible. It does not care for your readiness. It only reveals."

The artifact pulsed again, its light growing brighter. The figure began to dissolve, its form scattering like ash in the wind. *"Follow the light,"* it said, its voice fading with the shadows. *"Your path lies ahead."*

The artifact's glow intensified, casting beams of light that cut through the darkness. Aryan shielded his eyes, squinting against the brilliance. When the light dimmed, he saw a path stretching out from the clearing, its edges shimmering faintly.

He took a deep breath, steeling himself. "No turning back," he murmured, stepping onto the path.

The journey was disorienting. The ground beneath his feet felt solid yet ephemeral, as if he were walking on air. The landscape around him shifted constantly—one moment a dense forest, the next an endless plain.

And always, in the distance, a faint, glowing line: the Veil.

As Aryan approached the Veil, its presence became overwhelming. The air crackled with energy, and a deep hum resonated in his chest. The glowing line wasn't a barrier, as he had imagined, but a shimmering expanse that seemed to stretch infinitely in every direction.

He hesitated at the edge, the artifact thrumming in his hands. The Veil's light was hypnotic, its surface rippling like liquid gold.

"What happens if I cross it?" he wondered aloud.

The artifact pulsed once, as if in response.

Aryan took a deep breath, his thoughts racing. *What if the truth destroys me? What if it sets me free?*

Closing his eyes, he stepped forward.

The moment he touched the Veil, the world exploded into light. Images flashed before his eyes—memories, dreams, fragments of lives he had never lived. He saw himself standing on a mountain peak, a crowd cheering below. He saw himself alone in a desolate wasteland, the artifact shattered at his feet.

Voices echoed around him, overlapping and indistinct. One voice cut through the chaos, sharp and commanding: *"You must choose Aryan. What will you do with the truth?"*

The light faded, and Aryan found himself standing in a vast, empty space. Before him stood a mirror, its surface rippling like the Veil itself. Steeling himself, Aryan stepped closer.

***

# 14

# The Mirror's Edge

Aryan stood before the rippling mirror, his reflection shifting and elusive. It was as if the mirror knew him but refused to reveal itself fully. He felt his breath quicken, his palms damp against the artifact's surface.

*"You must choose,"* the shadowy figure's voice echoed in his memory.

But choose what? Aryan's thoughts raced. The mirror seemed alive, its surface pulsating in time with his heartbeat.

He reached out tentatively, his fingers brushing the liquid-like surface. The mirror rippled and pulled him in, swallowing him whole.

Aryan stumbled into a void, a boundless expanse of light and shadow interwoven. His footing felt unsteady, the ground both solid and intangible. The artifact in his hands began to hum, its patterns shifting and glowing.

"Where am I?" he murmured, his voice swallowed by the void.

A familiar voice answered, soft but resonant. "You stand at the edge of yourself."

Aryan spun around. The figure of his father stood before him, just as he remembered—tall, calm, and strong, with the faintest trace of a smile. But there was something else in his eyes, something Aryan had never seen before: sorrow.

"Father?" Aryan's voice cracked. He took a step forward, but his father raised a hand, halting him.

"You've come far," his father said. "But the path ahead demands more than courage. It demands clarity."

Aryan shook his head, emotions welling up. "Why didn't you tell me? About Kabir, the artifact... any of it?"

His father's gaze softened. "Because the truth isn't something you're told. It's something you earn."

Aryan's grip on the artifact tightened. "Then tell me now. What is the Veil? What happens if I cross it?"

His father's form flickered, as though struggling to hold itself together. "The Veil is a bridge, Aryan. It connects what is to what could be. But it is also a test. To cross it, you must confront the truth you fear most."

The void around them began to shift, forming shapes and scenes that felt eerily familiar. Aryan saw himself as a child, running through the fields near their home. He saw his mother, her laughter filling the air. And then he saw the moment he had tried so hard to bury: the night his father didn't return.

The scene played out before him with brutal clarity—the knock on the door, his mother's-stricken face, the message delivered by a man in a soldier's uniform. Aryan turned away, his chest tightening.

"Why are you showing me this?" he demanded.

"Because you carry it with you," his father said, stepping closer. "Your guilt, your anger—they shape every choice you make. To cross the Veil, you must let them go."

Aryan felt tears sting his eyes. "I don't know how," he whispered.

His father placed a hand on his shoulder, solid and warm. "The truth isn't about forgetting, Aryan. It's about accepting. You cannot change the past, but you can choose how it defines you."

The void began to glow brighter, the artifact in Aryan's hands vibrating with intensity. His father's form began to dissolve.

"Wait!" Aryan cried. "Don't go!"

His father smiled, his voice fading. "I'm always with you, Aryan. You just have to look."

The light engulfed him, and Aryan found himself back in the clearing, the artifact blazing in his hands. He felt a strange calm settle over him, the weight in his chest lifting ever so slightly.

The path to the Veil lay before him, clearer than ever. He took a deep breath and stepped forward, his father's words echoing in his mind. *"The truth isn't about forgetting. It's about accepting."*

***

# 15

# The Weight of Choices

The forest had transformed. Where once the trees were dark sentinels of mystery, they now stood luminous, their bark etched with faintly glowing symbols. The path before Aryan seemed alive, shifting subtly as though nudging him forward. Yet every step felt heavier, as if the ground itself tested his resolve.

The artifact pulsed faintly in his grip. Its glow no longer felt foreign; it was as if it mirrored his heartbeat, responding to his thoughts and fears.

"You're beginning to see," a voice echoed from the shadows ahead.

Aryan halted, his fingers tightening on the artifact. "Who's there?"

From the shifting light emerged a figure—not the shadowy enigma from the mirror but a woman cloaked in flowing silks, her eyes like pools of starlight. Her presence was both serene and unsettling, as if she carried the weight of countless truths.

"I am Kalyana," she said, her voice soft yet commanding. "Guardian of the Threshold."

Aryan stepped back, unsure of her intent. "Are you here to stop me?"

Kalyana smiled faintly. "No one can stop you but yourself. My role is to ensure that you understand the price of your choices."

She gestured to the path ahead, where the Veil shimmered faintly in the distance. "Each step you take toward the Veil brings you closer to truth, but it also carries a cost. Are you ready to bear it?"

Aryan frowned. "What kind of cost?"

Kalyana's gaze was steady, almost piercing. "The truth, Aryan, is not a gift. It is a burden. To see it is to change—irrevocably. You must decide if the clarity you seek is worth what you may lose."

Her words lingered, heavy in the air. Aryan looked down at the artifact, its surface swirling with patterns he couldn't quite decipher. He thought of his father's words, the memory of Kabir's teachings, the poem that now seemed to echo in every corner of his mind.

"What if I don't cross?" he asked, his voice barely above a whisper.

"Then you remain as you are," Kalyana said. "Unchanged, unbroken. But also unfulfilled. The Veil does not punish those who turn away; it simply waits for those willing to see."

Aryan hesitated, the weight of her words settling in his chest. He had always thought of truth as something to be pursued, an absolute to be attained. But now he wondered—was he chasing clarity, or running from the shadows of his past?

Kalyana stepped closer, her presence both comforting and intimidating. "The path you choose is yours alone, Aryan. But understand this: to cross the Veil is not to find answers. It is to face the questions you fear most. Are you ready to face yourself?"

Aryan closed his eyes, the artifact warm against his palm. The memories of his father, Kabir, and the mirror swirled in his mind. He thought of the poem's words, their cryptic message now tinged with meaning:

*"In shadows cast, in light revealed, the self is both the wound and shield."*

When he opened his eyes, Kalyana was gone. The path before him was clear, the Veil shimmering like a living thing.

Aryan took a deep breath and stepped forward. Each stride felt like an eternity, the air growing denser, the world around him dimming. As he approached the Veil, the artifact blazed with light, its patterns coalescing into a single, radiant symbol.

The Veil pulsed, its surface rippling like water. Aryan reached out, his hand trembling, the weight of his journey pressing down on him. For a moment, he hesitated, the enormity of the moment threatening to overwhelm him.

Then, with a deep breath, he stepped through.

***

# 16

# The Veil Beyond

The first sensation was weightlessness. Aryan floated, suspended in a space that defied understanding. The Veil's shimmering threads wrapped around him like tendrils of light, probing, testing, and whispering truths he wasn't ready to hear.

His mind felt fractured, as though he existed in a thousand places at once. He saw himself as a child, a man, a seeker, and something else—something he couldn't yet name. The artifact in his grip burned hot, anchoring him even as the currents of the Veil tried to pull him apart.

*"You have crossed, but do you carry the strength to remain?"*

The voice was not his father's, nor Kalyana's. It was vast, resonant, and carried the weight of ages.

Aryan struggled to speak, his voice lost in the endless expanse. "What… what is this place?"

*"This is the space between,"* the voice replied. *"The mirror to all that is and could be. You have sought truth, but truth is not given. It is revealed."*

As the voice faded, the Veil's light began to shift, solidifying into a landscape. Aryan found himself standing in a vast field, the grass shimmering like silver. The sky above was a swirling tapestry of stars, each one pulsating in rhythm with his heartbeat.

In the distance, a figure stood, shrouded in a glow that seemed to blur the edges of reality.

Aryan approached cautiously, the artifact still glowing faintly in his hand. As he neared, the figure resolved into a reflection of himself—yet not quite. This Aryan was older, his eyes carrying the weight of countless choices and their consequences.

The two regarded each other in silence, the air between them heavy with unspoken questions.

"Is this... me?" Aryan finally asked.

The older version of himself nodded. "I am you that might be. The choices you make here will shape the path ahead."

Aryan felt his throat tighten. "What choices? What do I need to do?"

The older Aryan stepped closer, his gaze intense. "The artifact you hold is more than a key. It is a mirror, a reflection of your soul. To wield its power, you must confront what you fear most—not the world's truths, but your own."

The ground beneath them shifted, and scenes began to play out like fractured memories. Aryan saw moments from his past: his father teaching him to hold a bow, Kabir's cryptic lessons, the nights he spent staring at the stars, yearning for something more.

But then the scenes darkened. He saw himself hesitating in moments that mattered, failing to act out of fear or doubt. He saw the pain in his mother's eyes when he refused to speak of his father. He saw the lives he could have touched but didn't, the opportunities lost to his uncertainty.

The older Aryan's voice cut through the chaos. "You carry these shadows with you, but they do not define you. What defines you is what you choose to do now."

The artifact in Aryan's hand began to pulse wildly, its light growing brighter. The older Aryan raised a hand, and the artifact's glow shifted, projecting two paths before them.

One path led back to the world Aryan knew—a place of familiarity and safety. The other path disappeared into darkness, its end unseen.

"You can return," the older Aryan said, his voice steady. "You can live your life as it is, untouched by the Veil's truths. Or you can step forward, into the unknown. But understand this: the unknown will change you, and not all who cross return whole."

Aryan's mind raced. The first path was tempting—a chance to escape the weight of the journey, to find peace in simplicity. But the second path called to him, its darkness both terrifying and exhilarating.

He turned to his older self. "What would you choose?"

The older Aryan smiled faintly. "It is not my choice to make. The man I exist because you dared to step forward. But whether you will become me—or someone else entirely—is up to you."

Aryan's grip on the artifact tightened. His heart pounded as he stared at the two paths, the weight of the moment pressing down on him.

Then, with a deep breath, he stepped toward the unknown.

The older Aryan's form began to dissolve, his voice echoing one last time. "Remember, the truth is not found. It is forged."

***

# 17

# The Burden of Worth

The path through the unknown was unlike anything Aryan had ever experienced. It was not dark as he'd expected, but instead a shifting mosaic of light and shadow. The ground beneath him rippled like water, each step sending echoes through the strange expanse.

The air carried whispers, faint and indistinct, as if voices from forgotten lives tried to reach him. Aryan clutched the artifact, its warmth steady in his hand, a comforting anchor in this uncharted realm.

As he walked, the whispers grew louder, forming words that seemed directed at him.

*"Why do you fear rejection?"*

Aryan froze. The voice wasn't like the others he'd heard—it was familiar, almost intimate, as though it came from within.

He looked around, but the landscape offered no answers. "I don't fear rejection," he said aloud, his voice uncertain even to his own ears.

The voice responded, its tone calm yet probing. *"Do you not? Then why do you carry the weight of others' opinions as though they define you?"*

The question struck a nerve. Aryan thought of his father, the expectations placed upon him as a child, the unspoken pressure to live up to a legacy he barely understood. He thought of Kabir, whose cryptic guidance always seemed to demand more than he felt capable of giving.

"Because I want to matter," Aryan admitted, his voice barely above a whisper. "I don't want to fail."

The whispers softened, as if acknowledging his vulnerability. Then, from the light and shadow ahead, a figure emerged. It was not the older Aryan from before but a version of himself younger, more innocent—untouched by the world's demands.

The younger Aryan looked at him with wide, curious eyes. "What does it mean to fail?" he asked.

Aryan hesitated. The question seemed simple, yet it felt impossible to answer. "It means... falling short. Letting people down. Losing their respect."

The younger Aryan tilted his head, frowning. "And if you lose their respect, does that make you less?"

Aryan opened his mouth to respond but found himself at a loss. The child continued, his voice soft but firm. "Why do you let them decide your worth? Doesn't that make you their prisoner?"

The words hit Aryan like a blow. He thought of the countless times he'd held himself back, afraid of disappointing others, afraid of what failure would say about him. How often had he shaped his actions—not for himself, but to meet the expectations of those around him?

The landscape began to shift again, the light and shadow resolving into scenes from Aryan's life. He saw moments when he'd been praised, his achievements celebrated by those around him. But then the scenes darkened, showing the cost of that praise—the sleepless nights, the constant pressure, the gnawing fear of losing it all.

One scene lingered longer than the others: a younger Aryan standing in the rain, clutching a broken arrow. He remembered the day clearly—his first failure in archery training. His father had said nothing, his silence heavier than any rebuke.

"That's when it started," Aryan realized aloud. "I equated failure with losing love. And I've been running from it ever since."

The younger Aryan stepped closer, his expression gentle. "But love isn't something you earn, is it? It's not a reward for success or a punishment for failure."

Aryan knelt, his grip on the artifact loosening as he met the child's gaze. "Then what is it?"

The child smiled faintly, a glimmer of wisdom in his innocent eyes. "It's something you carry, not something you chase. And it's time you learned to carry it for yourself."

The artifact in Aryan's hand began to glow brighter, its warmth spreading through him. For the first time, he felt its weight lessen, as though it no longer bore the burden of others' expectations.

As the younger Aryan faded back into the light, the whispers returned, softer now, almost like a lullaby.

*"You are not your successes, nor your failures. Your worth is your own—unchanging, unshaken."*

Aryan stood, his shoulders lighter, his steps surer. The path ahead remained uncertain, but he no longer feared it. The artifact pulsed in his hand, not as a weight but as a reminder—a reflection of the truths he was beginning to accept.

*** 

# 18

# The Labyrinth of Mirrors

The path twisted sharply, leading Aryan into a narrow corridor lined with mirrors. Their surfaces shimmered like liquid, reflecting not just his image but countless variations of himself—each one subtly different.

Some versions of Aryan stood taller, more confident, adorned in regal attire. Others appeared frail and worn, their eyes hollow with regret. The sight unsettled him, each reflection pulling at a thread in his mind, whispering of paths he had not taken and lives he could have lived.

The artifact vibrated faintly in his hand, its light dimming as if urging caution.

As he stepped deeper into the labyrinth, the mirrors began to ripple, their reflections shifting. Now he saw moments from his life replaying like scenes on a stage: his father's stern gaze during archery practice, his mother's quiet tears when he left home, and Kabir's cryptic words echoing in the still air.

*"A thousand lives in every choice."*

The voice startled Aryan. It was not his own but came from one of the mirrors. He turned to see a reflection of himself staring back, its expression cold and unyielding.

"You've come far," the reflection said, stepping out from the glass as if it were a doorway. "But have you truly made peace with the choices that brought you here?"

Aryan instinctively raised the artifact, its light flickering to life. "Who are you?"

The figure smirked. "I'm you—or rather, you that clings to every regret, every missed opportunity, every failure you've refused to accept."

The words struck Aryan like a physical blow. He tightened his grip on the artifact, his voice firm. "I've faced my fears. I know my worth now."

"Do you?" the reflection countered, stepping closer. "Or are you just telling yourself that because it's easier than looking at the truth?"

The labyrinth around them darkened, the mirrors warping into jagged shards. Aryan's reflection raised a hand, and the scene shifted to a memory Aryan had long buried.

He saw himself standing on the edge of a battlefield, his bow trembling in his hands. A younger warrior lay wounded nearby, his cries for help drowned by the chaos of the fight. Aryan remembered the moment vividly—the hesitation, the fear that froze him in place. He had turned away, leaving the man to his fate.

"You tell yourself it wasn't your fault," the reflection said, its tone cutting. "That you weren't ready, that you couldn't have made a difference. But the truth is, you were afraid. And that fear cost a life."

Aryan's chest tightened. The memory had haunted him for years, though he had tried to justify it, to rationalize his actions. Now, faced with it directly, he felt the weight of his choices anew.

"I was afraid," Aryan admitted, his voice breaking. "I failed him."

The reflection's gaze softened, its voice losing its edge. "Failure isn't the end, Aryan. But denying it? That's what keeps you trapped."

The artifact pulsed in his hand, its light growing brighter. Aryan felt its warmth spreading through him, dispelling the cold grip of guilt.

The reflection stepped back, nodding as the mirrors around them began to repair themselves, their surfaces smoothing into calm pools of light.

"Remember this," the reflection said, its voice fading. "Your failures shape you, but they do not define you. Carry their lessons, not their weight."

Aryan watched as the figure dissolved into the light, leaving him alone once more. The labyrinth shifted, its walls parting to reveal a new path ahead.

***

# 19

# The Silent Burden

The path beyond the labyrinth was silent, almost oppressively so. Aryan walked with measured steps; the artifact steady in his grip. The light it emitted had shifted, now softer and more golden, like the first rays of dawn.

Ahead, a towering structure emerged from the mist—a crumbling temple carved from black stone; its walls etched with symbols Aryan couldn't decipher. The air around it was heavy, filled with the weight of something ancient and unspoken.

As he approached, the doors of the temple creaked open on their own, revealing a dim interior lit by flickering torches. A voice, deep and resonant, echoed from within.

*"Enter, bearer of the light. The past calls you forward."*

Aryan hesitated but stepped inside. The air was thick with the scent of burning incense, and the flickering flames cast shifting shadows on the walls. At the centre of the room stood a circular pool of water, its surface unnaturally still.

Around the pool were statues—figures of warriors, scholars, and wanderers, each holding an object that seemed to shimmer with faint light. Aryan felt drawn to the pool, its surface reflecting not the room around it but a star-filled sky.

The voice spoke again, this time softer, almost a whisper.

*"Touch the water and see what was lost."*

Aryan knelt by the pool, the artifact glowing faintly in his hand. As he dipped his fingers into the water, the surface rippled, and the stars gave way to a scene from the past.

He saw a bustling village, its streets alive with activity. At the centre of it all stood a younger version of his father, speaking passionately to a group of villagers. Aryan's breath caught in his throat—he had never seen his father so alive, so full of purpose.

The vision shifted, showing his father leading a group of people into the wilderness, their faces marked by hope and determination. But then came the storm—the skies darkened, and chaos erupted. The group was scattered, and his father stood alone, clutching an object that looked strikingly similar to Aryan's artifact.

The vision ended abruptly, the water stilling once more.

Aryan sat back, his mind racing. "This is his legacy," he murmured, his voice tinged with awe and sorrow. "This was his burden."

The voice returned, this time more insistent. *"And now it is yours. But do you understand what it means to carry it?"*

Aryan looked at the statues surrounding the pool, their silent forms seeming to watch him. Each figure had carried something—a responsibility, a truth, a burden. Some had succeeded, others had failed, but all had left their mark on the world.

"What if I'm not ready?" Aryan asked, his voice barely above a whisper. The torches flared, and the voice replied, *"No one is ever ready. But readiness is not the measure of worth—it is the willingness to act despite the weight of uncertainty."*

The artifact in Aryan's hand began to hum, its light growing stronger. He felt a warmth spreading through him, mingling with a deep sense of responsibility. The journey was no longer just about him—it was about honouring the sacrifices of those who had come before and preparing the way for those who would come after.

The statues seemed to nod in silent agreement as the water in the pool shimmered once more. This time, it showed Aryan's own face, but not as he was now. He looked older, wiser, and stronger—a reflection of what he could become if he chose to embrace his path fully.

Aryan rose to his feet, his grip on the artifact firm. "I may not be ready," he said, his voice steady. "But I will not turn away."

The temple seemed to respond, its walls vibrating with a low hum. The torches dimmed, and the heavy doors opened once more, revealing the path ahead.

As Aryan stepped out into the open air, he felt a renewed sense of purpose. The whispers of doubt that had once plagued him were quieter now, replaced by a calm determination. The journey was far from over, but for the first time, he felt truly aligned with the path he was meant to walk.

*** 

# 20

# The Weaving of Fates

The terrain ahead was unlike anything Aryan had encountered before—a vast expanse of threads, golden and silver, stretched across the horizon. They wove and unwound in patterns that seemed random at first but, on closer inspection, revealed a deeper logic. The air buzzed faintly, as if the threads carried whispers of lives connected through time and space.

The artifact pulsed faintly in his hand, its glow resonating with the threads, as though urging him forward.

Stepping cautiously onto the field, Aryan noticed how the threads moved. Each one vibrated to a rhythm of its own, but together, they created a symphony—an intricate melody of fate, choice, and consequence. He felt himself drawn to one of the golden threads that shimmered brighter than the rest.

The moment he touched it, a cascade of images flooded his mind. He saw faces—some familiar, some not. His father, Kabir, the young warrior he had failed to save, and even people he had yet to meet. The images came with feelings: joy, regret, fear, and love, each one tied to a decision he had made or would make.

The ground beneath him shifted, and Aryan found himself standing in a dimly lit chamber. At its centre sat a figure cloaked in silver, their face obscured by a veil that shimmered like the threads outside.

"You have entered the Loom of Eternity," the figure said, their voice calm and resonant. "Here, all lives intertwine, and all choices converge."

Aryan hesitated, his grip on the artifact tightening. "What is my role in this? Why am I here?"

The figure gestured toward the golden thread Aryan had touched. "You are here to understand. Each thread is a life, and each knot is a choice. Your choices do not exist in isolation— they ripple through the weave, binding and unbinding fates."

The figure motioned for Aryan to follow, leading him deeper into the chamber where the threads grew denser, their patterns more intricate.

"Your journey has unravelled many threads, some intentionally, others by chance. But you must ask yourself: what are you weaving? A tapestry of hope, or one of despair?"

Aryan felt a pang of doubt. "How can I know? Every choice feels like a step into the unknown."

The figure turned, their veiled face somehow exuding both wisdom and kindness. "You cannot always know. But you can choose with intention, with understanding. The artifact you carry is not just a key—it is a mirror, reflecting the truths you must face."

The artifact pulsed again, brighter now, and Aryan saw another vision. This time, it showed him at a crossroads, his younger self hesitating while others around him moved with certainty.

"You have always feared the permanence of your decisions," the figure said. "But fear does not undo the knots already tied. It only keeps you from weaving what is yet to come."

Aryan looked at the threads surrounding him, their complexity daunting yet mesmerizing. For the first time, he felt a sense of agency—not as a passive traveller on this journey, but as a weaver of his own destiny.

The figure stepped back, their form blending into the shimmering threads. "Remember, Aryan, every thread is connected. Your choices shape not only your fate but the fates of others. Choose wisely, but do not fear choosing."

As the figure disappeared, the chamber dissolved into light, and Aryan found himself back on the field of threads. The artifact in his hand shone with a steady glow, its warmth spreading through him.

He took a deep breath and began to walk forward, each step filled with newfound purpose. The threads shifted around him, creating paths where there were none, as though the world itself was responding to his resolve.

***

# 21

# Threads of Choice

The threads of the Loom shimmered faintly in Aryan's mind as he descended into the mist-covered valley. The memory of the figure's parting words lingered: *Every thread is connected. Choose wisely, but do not fear choosing.*

The valley stretched wide before him, a barren yet strangely alive expanse where the air seemed to hum with quiet anticipation. The artifact in his hand grew warmer as he neared a solitary stone pedestal at the valley's centre. It was unadorned, ancient, and unyielding, its surface etched with lines that mirrored the patterns of the Loom.

Aryan hesitated. Every step here felt weighted, as though the ground itself bore witness to his journey and judged his worth. The weight of choices past and yet to come pressed against his chest.

He reached the pedestal and placed the artifact atop it. The glow intensified, casting golden light over the valley. The light rippled outward, illuminating three paths that had been invisible moments before. Each path was distinct, veiled in its own mystery.

The first was narrow, with steep, jagged edges. It led upward to a high peak where faint flames flickered in the distance. The second wound gently through a lush forest, its canopy whispering promises of respite. The third was shrouded in fog, its end invisible, but it pulsed faintly as though alive.

A voice, neither Kabir's nor his own, resonated from the artifact. "Every path carries a burden. Every choice shapes the weave. Which will you claim?"

Aryan's mind raced. The first path whispered of trials and challenges, a chance to prove his strength but at the risk of isolation. The second promised comfort and clarity, but its ease made him question its cost. The third, cloaked in uncertainty, unnerved him the most, yet it stirred something deeper—a call not to answers, but to discovery.

He thought of Kabir's teachings. *The path that frightens you most often holds the greatest truth.*

He stepped toward the fog-covered path. The moment his foot touched it, the world shifted. The valley disappeared, replaced by an endless corridor of mirrors.

In each mirror, Aryan saw a reflection—not of himself as he was, but as he could be.

One showed him triumphant, crowned in light, holding the artifact aloft as people cheered his name. Another displayed him sitting alone in a vast library, the artifact forgotten on a dusty shelf. The third was the hardest to face. It showed Aryan kneeling in defeat, the artifact shattered at his feet, yet his eyes glimmered with peace.

He reached out to the third reflection, drawn to the rawness of it. The moment his fingers brushed the glass, the corridor melted away, and he was back in the valley. But the artifact had changed—it was no longer smooth and polished. Cracks ran along its surface, glowing faintly.

The voice returned, softer now. "The thread of truth is rarely unbroken. You chose uncertainty, and in doing so, you chose growth."

As Aryan left the valley, the threads of the Loom appeared faintly in the sky above him, a reminder of the interconnected paths he had glimpsed. For the first time, he felt not the weight of his choices, but the freedom to make them.

The journey ahead was no clearer, but the fear that had shadowed him since the beginning had begun to lift.

*** 

# 22

# The Burden's Shadow

The mist clung to Aryan as he climbed the winding trail out of the valley. The faint cracks on the artifact radiated a warmth that alternated between reassuring and unsettling. It felt alive in a way it hadn't before, as if it bore silent witness to his choices and now shared his burdens.

The world above the valley unfolded with stark contrast. Aryan found himself in a dense, untamed forest where sunlight barely pierced the thick canopy. The air smelled of damp earth and pine, and the distant chirping of birds was the only sound, aside from the crunch of leaves underfoot.

Kabir had once described such a place in one of his stories. *"The forest tests more than your resolve; it tests your willingness to confront the unseen. Fear does not always announce itself—it waits quietly, disguised as safety."* Aryan had laughed at the time, dismissing it as one of Kabir's cryptic lessons. Now, as the dense foliage seemed to close in around him, he understood.

Hours passed, or so it seemed, as Aryan navigated the forest's winding paths. Each turn felt deliberately ambiguous, as if the forest itself was testing his resolve.

The Weave - *Threads of Choices and Connections*

The first sign of change came when he stumbled upon a clearing. In its centre stood a weathered statue, partially consumed by moss and vines. It depicted a man kneeling with hands outstretched, cradling an unseen object. The man's face was carved with such precision that Aryan could see the anguish etched into his features.

Beneath the statue lay a plaque, the words barely legible beneath centuries of erosion. Aryan brushed away the dirt and read aloud:

*"To bear the weight of what cannot be changed is the mark of a true soul."*

The artifact grew heavier in his hand as he absorbed the words. His thoughts flickered to the faces of those he had lost: his father, the young warrior, even strangers whose lives had been caught in the crossfire of his journey. Each memory brought with it a pang of guilt. Could he truly bear their weight and still move forward?

Before he could ponder further, the forest darkened unnaturally, and the air grew cold. Shadows stretched from the trees, pooling into a single, towering form.

The creature that emerged was unlike anything Aryan had encountered. Its body was formless, shifting between solid and mist, its eyes burning with an intense, malevolent glow. It spoke, its voice resonating as if carried on the wind:

*"You carry their echoes, their pain. But can you bear the truth?"*

Aryan froze, clutching the artifact. The creature did not attack but circled him, its presence oppressive.

"Who are you?" Aryan demanded, though his voice wavered.

*"I am the shadow of your choices, the weight you refuse to release. Show me your strength or be consumed by regret."*

The forest blurred, and suddenly Aryan was surrounded by images—fragments of his past failures. The warrior's lifeless eyes stared at him, Kabir's unspoken disappointment lingered, and his father's voice echoed faintly: *"Will you carry my legacy, or let it crumble?"*

Aryan dropped to his knees, overwhelmed. The artifact in his hand pulsed, and he realized the cracks were growing, glowing brighter with each heartbeat.

"You're wrong," Aryan said, his voice breaking but resolute. "I don't refuse the weight—I carry it because I must. Not to be consumed by it, but to learn from it."

The creature stopped circling, its form flickering as if uncertain. Aryan rose, the artifact glowing steadily in his hand.

"You can haunt me with these failures," Aryan continued, his voice gaining strength. "But they're part of me. Without them, I wouldn't be standing here. I won't run from them anymore."

The creature's glowing eyes dimmed. It let out a low, guttural sound that might have been a laugh or a sigh. *"We shall see, Aryan. The threads you weave are fragile yet. But for now, you pass."*

The creature dissolved, leaving behind a single thread of shimmering light suspended in the air. Aryan reached out hesitantly, and as his fingers closed around it, a sudden wave of clarity washed over him.

The thread seemed to merge with the artifact, and the cracks sealed themselves faintly, though not completely. The warmth in his hand steadied, as if the artifact was now more in tune with him.

As Aryan emerged from the forest hours later, the world seemed brighter, the air fresher. He realized that the forest had not been a test of strength, but of acceptance. He had confronted his shadows and emerged not unscarred, but unbroken.

The path ahead beckoned, and Aryan knew the choices would only grow harder. But for the first time in his journey, he felt not the weight of his failures, but the strength they had given him.

***

# 23

# The Unseen Loom

The path wound upward now, away from the dense forest and into rocky terrain where the air thinned and the sky seemed closer. Aryan's legs ached with every step, but the steady hum of the artifact in his hand kept him moving.

Above him, jagged peaks loomed, their tops veiled in swirling clouds. The trail twisted sharply at times, and loose stones made each step a test of balance. Yet, as he climbed higher, Aryan felt a curious stillness settling over him—a quietness not of exhaustion but of anticipation.

He paused at a narrow ledge, leaning against the cliff face to catch his breath. Looking out over the expanse below, he saw the faint shimmer of the valley and the forest he had left behind. Each step of the journey felt impossibly far now, yet they were all connected, threads in a vast tapestry he couldn't yet see fully.

*"How much further, and what waits for me?"* he wondered aloud.

As if in response, the artifact pulsed. A soft light emerged from its surface, spilling into the air like liquid gold. The light wove itself into thin lines that stretched into the sky, forming an intricate web above him.

Aryan stared in awe. It wasn't the first time the artifact had shown him something mysterious, but this was different. The web shifted constantly, threads intertwining and separating, patterns emerging only to dissolve again.

"You see it now," a voice said behind him.

Aryan spun around, his grip tightening on the artifact. A woman stood a few paces away, her figure shrouded in a flowing gray cloak. Her face was weathered, with deep lines that spoke of both hardship and wisdom. Yet her eyes sparkled with an almost youthful vitality.

"Who are you?" Aryan asked cautiously.

She stepped closer, her movements deliberate but unthreatening. "A weaver," she said simply. "As are you."

The woman extended her hand, and Aryan noticed a faint thread running from her fingertips into the shimmering web above. It pulsed faintly, as though alive.

"Every thread you see belongs to someone," she explained. "Every choice, every thought, every act—woven into the Loom of Existence." She gestured toward Aryan's artifact. "And that is not just a relic. It's a spindle, meant to guide your weaving."

Aryan glanced at the artifact, now glowing faintly in his hand. "You're saying this... connects to the Loom?"

She nodded. "And more. It doesn't just connect—it shapes. With every choice you've made, every fear you've faced, you've been weaving your own thread into the greater tapestry."

Aryan frowned, his mind spinning. "If that's true, then what happens if someone chooses wrongly? Or if they refuse to act?"

The woman's smile was faint but knowing. "A thread left unchosen is a thread left untwined. It dangles, fraying, until it becomes part of someone else's weave. But a wrong choice?" She stepped closer, her gaze piercing. "There's no such thing. Every thread finds its place, even if the weaver doesn't see it at first."

The weight of her words settled over Aryan like the mist that clung to the peaks. He thought of his father, of Kabir, and of the lives he had affected on this journey. How many threads had he intertwined with his own without realizing it?

"Why show me this now?" Aryan asked. "What am I supposed to do?"

She pointed to the peaks above. "Because your choices will soon affect not just your thread but the weave itself. The Loom is fragile, Aryan. Strands are unravelling, knots tightening where they shouldn't. You've seen it—the cracks in the world, the shadow that haunts you. They're all symptoms of imbalance."

Aryan's grip tightened on the artifact. "And you think I can fix it?"

The woman's smile softened. "Not alone. But your thread is unique, Aryan. It bridges past and present, loss and hope. What you do next will ripple outward in ways even I cannot foresee."

She stepped back, her form beginning to blur at the edges. "Climb, Aryan. The Loom awaits you."

"Wait!" he called, but she was already gone, her thread dissolving into the golden web.

For a moment, Aryan stood frozen, the weight of her words pressing on him. Then he looked up toward the peaks, where the path vanished into the clouds. He adjusted his pack and started forward, the artifact steady in his hand.

The climb grew steeper, the air colder. Yet Aryan pressed on, each step feeling like a thread being woven into something larger. He couldn't see the Loom yet, but he felt its presence—a vast, unseen force pulling him forward.

And for the first time, he began to understand that his journey was not just about discovery, but about creation.

***

# 24

# Threads of Revelation

The air grew thinner as Aryan approached the summit, the clouds parting to reveal a vast plateau. The space felt otherworldly, as if it were suspended between realms. The ground beneath him shimmered faintly, reflecting the sky above. In the centre of the plateau, an ancient structure stood—a circular dais with intricate carvings etched into its surface.

The artifact in Aryan's hand pulsed more intensely than ever before, as if urging him onward. He stepped onto the dais, and the world seemed to shift. The carvings beneath him glowed, tracing lines that connected to the artifact and extended outward in every direction, forming a massive, intricate web across the plateau.

As Aryan stood at the centre, the web came alive, each thread glowing in succession. The threads stretched into the sky, converging at a single point above him where a pulsating orb of light hovered. The sight was overwhelming—a kaleidoscope of colours and patterns, each thread vibrating with energy.

Suddenly, a voice resonated from the orb, neither male nor female, but a harmonious blend of tones.

The Weave - *Threads of Choices and Connections*

*"You stand at the heart of the Loom, Aryan. The choices you've made, the lives you've touched—all have led you here."*

Aryan swallowed hard. "If this is the Loom, then why does it feel like it's falling apart? The woman said it's fragile, that threads are unravelling."

The voice replied, its tone sombre. *"The Loom reflects the balance of existence. Every choice, every consequence, weaves a thread. But imbalance has crept into the weave—choices made out of fear, threads severed too soon. The artifact you carry holds the power to restore what has been broken."*

Aryan looked down at the artifact. "But I don't understand how. All I've done is survive. I've made mistakes, hurt people... How can I possibly fix this?"

The orb pulsed, and images appeared in the air around him—moments from his journey. His father's teachings, Kabir's guidance, the shadowy creature in the forest, the weaver's cryptic warnings. Each memory was a thread, connecting to the artifact and to him.

*"You have already begun,"* the voice said. *"The artifact is not just a tool; it is a mirror. It reflects the strength you've found in your failures, the resolve you've forged in your pain. To mend the Loom, you must not erase the past but weave it into something new."*

A sudden rumble shook the plateau, and Aryan looked up to see threads snapping one by one, their light extinguished. The orb dimmed, its glow flickering.

*"The unravelling accelerates,"* the voice warned. *"A choice must be made."*

A figure emerged from the shadows at the edge of the plateau. It was the shadow creature, its form more defined now, its eyes burning with intensity.

And so, he walked on, ready to face whatever lay ahead.

*"He cannot mend what he does not fully understand,"* the creature said, its voice dripping with malice. *"You would have him patch the Loom blindly, only for it to tear again."*

The orb's light flared. *"His journey has prepared him. He carries the knowledge within."*

The creature sneered. *"Knowledge is not enough. Let him face the truth of his own thread. Only then can he claim the right to shape the Loom."*

The creature waved a hand, and a single thread descended from the orb, glowing brighter than the rest. Aryan instinctively knew it was his. The thread shimmered with moments of light and darkness, victories and losses, love and regret.

"Why show me this?" Aryan asked, his voice trembling.

*"To test your resolve,"* the creature replied. *"Do you see a thread worthy of the Loom, or one that should be severed to spare the weave further harm?"*

The question struck Aryan like a blow. He thought of every mistake he'd made, every life he'd failed to save. The thread pulsed as if awaiting his judgment.

The orb's voice softened. *"Do not judge your thread by its flaws alone. Every thread is imperfect, yet together they create something greater. The choice is yours, Aryan: embrace your thread or reject it. But understand this—your choice will ripple through the Loom."*

Aryan closed his eyes, the weight of the moment pressing down on him. The artifact in his hand grew warm, its light steady and unwavering.

"I've spent so long running from my failures," he said, his voice steady despite the storm of emotions within him. "But they've shaped me as much as my victories. My thread isn't perfect, but it's mine. And I won't let it be cut."

The creature hissed, but the orb flared brightly, silencing it. The thread rose back into the web, its light stronger than before. The snapping threads around Aryan began to reconnect, their light weaving into new patterns.

*"The Loom accepts your choice,"* the orb said. *"But your journey is not yet over. The balance must still be restored, and the artifact holds the key."*

The creature retreated, its form dissolving into the shadows. Aryan stood alone on the dais, the web around him glowing with renewed vigour. The artifact in his hand felt lighter, its warmth a reminder of the path he had chosen. As the light of the Loom began to fade, Aryan felt a surge of determination. The journey ahead was uncertain, but for the first time, he felt truly ready to face it.

***

# 25

# The Fractured Path

The descent from the plateau was marked by an eerie stillness. The weight of Aryan's decision lingered in the air, the warmth of the artifact a constant reminder of the journey ahead. As he traversed the narrow path back into the forest, the landscape seemed to shift. The trees stood taller, their branches intertwining to form a canopy that filtered the sunlight into shards of gold.

But beneath this beauty lay a tension, as though the forest itself was holding its breath. Aryan felt it in the rustling leaves and the faint tremors underfoot. The Loom might have begun to heal, but its balance was far from secure.

Hours into his journey, Aryan came across a small clearing. In its centre stood a dilapidated shrine, its stones weathered by time. A faint glow emanated from its core, drawing him closer. As he approached, he noticed carvings on the shrine's surface—symbols that mirrored those on the artifact.

Placing the artifact on the shrine, Aryan felt a surge of energy. The carvings illuminated, and a projection of Kabir appeared before him, translucent but vibrant.

"Kabir?" Aryan whispered, his voice thick with emotion.

Kabir smiled, his expression both warm and weary. "I see you've made it this far, Aryan. The Loom responded to your choice, but the balance it seeks demands more than courage."

"What more could it ask of me?" Aryan asked, his voice tinged with frustration.

"Understanding," Kabir replied. "The threads of existence are interconnected, but their true strength lies in unity. To restore the Loom, you must not only protect your own thread but also mend the broken connections around you."

The projection shifted, and Aryan saw visions of people he had encountered on his journey: the merchant who had sheltered him, the woman in the village who spoke of the Loom's fragility, even the shadow creature that had challenged him. Each thread glowed faintly, their ends frayed and untethered.

"These are the threads you've touched," Kabir explained. "Some you've strengthened, others you've weakened—intentionally or not. The Loom cannot heal while these connections remain fractured."

Aryan stared at the threads, guilt gnawing at him. "How do I fix this? I can't undo the past."

"You don't need to," Kabir said gently. "But you must take responsibility for the choices you've made. Seek out these threads, mend what you can, and accept what you cannot."

The glow from the shrine began to fade, and Kabir's image flickered.

"Wait!" Aryan called out. "I don't know where to start!"

Kabir's voice echoed faintly as the vision dissolved. "Trust the artifact—it will guide you. And remember, Aryan: the Loom thrives not on perfection, but on the strength of connection."

The shrine felt dark, leaving Aryan alone once more. He picked up the artifact, its light pulsing steadily, and turned back toward the forest.

As he walked, the artifact began to emit faint whispers, guiding him toward unseen paths. Each step brought him closer to another thread, another story, another chance to mend what was broken.

Aryan knew the road ahead would be fraught with challenges, but Kabir's words resonated within him. The journey was no longer just about the Loom or the artifact—it was about the lives intertwined with his own and the meaning they brought to the weave of existence.

***

# 26

# Frayed Connections

The whispers grew louder as Aryan continued through the forest. They weren't chaotic or dissonant but layered and rhythmic, like voices from different moments in time speaking in unison. Each whisper seemed to carry a memory, a fragment of emotion, pulling him toward unseen destinations.

He came upon a fork in the path. The artifact pulsed, the light pointing him toward the left trail. Aryan hesitated, glancing down the right path. It was darker, the trees twisted and ominous, as though warning him away.

"Is this trust or blind faith?" he muttered. But the artifact pulsed again, insistent. With a deep breath, he turned left.

The trail led to a small clearing where the air shimmered, heavy with energy. In the centre stood a young man, no older than Aryan, holding a bow carved with intricate patterns. His shoulders were slumped, and his face was etched with frustration.

Aryan approached cautiously. "Are you lost?"

The man turned sharply, his grip on the bow tightening. "Who are you?"

"My name is Aryan. I mean no harm."

The man studied him for a moment, then sighed, lowering the bow. "I don't know if I'm lost or just stuck. The Loom brought me here, but now... nothing makes sense."

Aryan's interest piqued. "You know about the Loom?"

"I've lived my whole life following its threads," the man said bitterly. "But no matter how much I try to honour it, nothing I do seems to matter. The threads I protect keep breaking."

Aryan felt a pang of recognition. "I've felt that way too. Like every step forward is undone by something I can't control. But maybe the point isn't control—it's connection."

The man looked sceptical. "And how do you rebuild something that's already broken?"

Aryan held up the artifact, its light casting a warm glow over the clearing. "You don't rebuild it alone. Let me help."

The artifact pulsed, and a thread descended from the sky, glowing faintly. Aryan realized it was connected to the man before him. The thread was frayed and uneven, but its core still pulsed with light.

"Your thread," Aryan said softly. "It's not broken—it's waiting."

The man stared at the thread, his expression softening. "Waiting for what?"

"For you to believe in it again," Aryan said. "Every thread has a purpose, even if we can't always see it. If the Loom brought you here, then it's not done with you yet."

The man hesitated, then reached out to touch the thread. The moment his fingers brushed it, the thread glowed brighter, its frayed edges smoothing. A wave of energy surged through the clearing, and the artifact in Aryan's hand pulsed in harmony.

The man looked at Aryan, a glimmer of hope in his eyes. "Thank you. I think... I think I understand now."

Aryan nodded. "You're not alone in this. None of us are."

As the man disappeared into the forest, Aryan felt a sense of quiet triumph. The artifact's whispers grew softer, guiding him toward the next thread.

For the first time, Aryan understood what Kabir had meant. Mending the Loom wasn't just about the artifact or the threads—it was about the people connected to them.

And so, he continued, each step bringing him closer to the balance he sought to restore.

***

# 27

# The Loom's Whisper

The forest thinned as Aryan pressed on, giving way to rolling hills bathed in the golden light of a setting sun. The artifact in his hand hummed softly, guiding him toward an isolated village nestled at the base of the hills. Smoke rose lazily from chimneys, and the faint sound of laughter and conversation carried on the breeze.

For a moment, Aryan hesitated. The sight of ordinary life—people who seemed untouched by the Loom's unravelling—was both comforting and disconcerting. Could they feel the imbalance creeping through the threads of existence, or were they blissfully unaware?

The artifact pulsed, drawing him forward. Aryan adjusted his pack and descended the hill, the weight of his purpose settling on his shoulders once more.

As he entered the village, curious eyes followed him. Children darted behind carts, peeking out to catch a glimpse of the stranger. An older man, tall and wiry, approached, wiping his hands on a cloth.

"Welcome, traveller," the man said, his tone cautious but polite. "What brings you to Elmshaven?"

Aryan glanced around, noting the wear on the buildings and the quiet tension in the villagers' faces. "I'm searching for something," he replied, choosing his words carefully. "I was guided here."

The man studied him for a moment before nodding. "Then perhaps the Loom has its reasons. Come, we don't turn away those in need."

The villagers gathered in a modest hall; its walls adorned with faded tapestries. Aryan sat among them, listening as they shared stories of their struggles. Crops had withered inexplicably, livestock had fallen ill, and the once-bustling market had dwindled to a shadow of its former self.

"We've tried everything," an elderly woman said, her voice heavy with despair. "Offerings, prayers, even leaving the land fallow. But it's as if the world itself has turned against us."

Aryan glanced at the artifact, its glow faint but steady. The threads were fraying here—he could feel it.

"I think I can help," he said finally, his voice steady. "But I'll need your trust."

The villagers exchanged wary glances, but the elder nodded. "If the Loom brought you here, we'll trust its guidance. Tell us what you need."

Aryan stood and raised the artifact, its light illuminating the hall. "This will show me what must be mended. But the threads I weave will require your strength and belief."

The artifact pulsed, and the air grew heavy with energy. Threads of light began to appear, weaving through the hall and into the villagers themselves. Aryan saw their connections—some bright and taut, others dim and frayed.

One thread caught his attention. It led to a young girl sitting silently in the corner, her gaze fixed on the floor. Her thread was thin, its light barely flickering.

Aryan knelt before the girl, offering her a gentle smile. "What's your name?"

"Lila," she whispered, her voice trembling.

He glanced at her thread, sensing the weight of something unspoken. "Lila, your thread is important. It connects to so many others here. But it's weak because something is holding it back. Can you tell me what it is?"

Tears welled in her eyes, and she shook her head. The elder stepped forward, his expression grave. "Lila hasn't spoken much since her parents passed last year. She's carried the burden of their loss alone."

Aryan's chest tightened. He thought of his own father, the weight of his absence a constant shadow. He reached for her hand, his voice soft. "Lila, I know what it feels like to lose someone you love. But the memories of those we've lost can make our threads stronger, not weaker. Will you let me help you?"

Lila hesitated, then nodded, her small hand clutching his. The artifact pulsed brightly, and her thread glowed stronger. Aryan felt the energy shift, a warmth spreading through the room as other threads began to brighten in response.

The villagers watched in awe as the artifact wove the threads together, their connections growing steadier. The room seemed to hum with renewed vitality, and Aryan saw the tension in their faces begin to lift.

As the light faded, Lila looked up at him, a faint smile on her lips. "Thank you," she whispered.

The elder approached, his voice filled with gratitude. "You've given us hope, Aryan. Whatever journey you're on, may the Loom guide you."

Aryan nodded, the weight on his shoulders feeling lighter. "The Loom isn't just threads and patterns—it's all of us. Strengthening your connections will strengthen the whole."

As he left the village, the artifact glowed brighter, its hum resonating with the renewed energy around him. Aryan knew the journey ahead would hold greater challenges, but this moment reminded him why he continued to walk this path.

***

# 28

# Beneath the Veil

The path ahead twisted sharply, flanked by jagged cliffs that loomed high above Aryan's head. A chill hung in the air, not from the weather, but from something deeper, something unseen. The artifact in his hand was subdued now, its light dim, as though it, too, hesitated to move forward.

For hours, Aryan had followed its faint pull, each step taking him closer to the source of a new disturbance. But this time, the weight of the journey felt heavier, as if the threads themselves resisted his approach.

As night fell, Aryan reached the mouth of a cavern carved into the cliffside. Its entrance was wide and yawning, the darkness within broken only by faint glimmers of light, like starlight caught in a web. The artifact's hum grew stronger, vibrating against his palm.

He stepped inside cautiously, his breath echoing softly against the walls. The cavern was vast, with stalactites hanging like frozen daggers. At its centre stood a stone pedestal, atop which rested a shimmering orb. Threads of light swirled around it, their movement frantic and chaotic.

Aryan's chest tightened as he stepped closer. The threads here weren't just frayed—they were severed, their loose ends writhing in agony.

From the shadows, a voice emerged, low and resonant. "You've come far, Aryan, but you do not belong here."

Aryan froze, his eyes darting to the darkness beyond the pedestal. A figure stepped into the dim light, cloaked in black. Their face was obscured, but their presence radiated an unsettling calm.

"Who are you?" Aryan asked, his voice steady despite the unease curling in his gut.

The figure tilted their head, as if amused. "I am the Keeper of the Veil. And you, child of the Loom, tread on dangerous ground."

Aryan tightened his grip on the artifact. "The threads here are broken. I'm here to mend them."

The Keeper laughed, the sound echoing hollowly. "Mend? You speak as if you understand the Loom, but you've seen only fragments. Do you know what happens when a thread is forced to reconnect? When a weave is bent to your will?"

Aryan faltered, his mind flashing back to the village, to Lila's fragile thread and the pain it carried. He thought of his father, of the unanswered questions and buried grief.

"I mend what I can," he replied. "Because if I don't, the Loom will fall apart."

The Keeper stepped closer, their movements unnervingly smooth. "The Loom is not yours to save, nor mine to destroy. It is a balance; one you've disrupted by your meddling."

The threads around the orb writhed more violently, their light flickering as if in pain. Aryan felt their energy, a mix of anguish and desperation. He stepped toward the pedestal, but the Keeper raised a hand, and the air grew heavy.

"Do you truly believe you are the Loom's saviour?" the Keeper asked, their tone sharper now. "Look around you. These threads were torn because of your actions elsewhere. Every choice you make ripples outward, pulling threads too tightly, tearing them apart."

Aryan's heart pounded. "If I don't act, they'll unravel completely. What would you have me do? Stand by and let it all collapse?"

The Keeper's silence was deafening. Then, with a measured calm, they said, "Perhaps the Loom must collapse for something new to rise."

The words hung in the air, and Aryan felt the weight of them settle in his chest. Doubt crept into his mind, whispering insidious questions. Was he truly mending the Loom, or was he weaving it into something it was never meant to be?

He looked at the artifact, its light pulsing weakly, and then at the orb. The threads around it seemed to reach for him, pleading silently.

"What do you want me to do?" Aryan asked, his voice barely above a whisper.

The Keeper stepped aside, their form dissolving into the shadows. "That is for you to decide. But know this—every thread you touch changes the Loom. Not all change is good."

Aryan approached the pedestal, his steps measured. The threads brushed against his skin, their touch electric and alive. He raised the artifact, its light growing brighter, and felt the threads respond. Slowly, carefully, he began to weave them together, their chaotic movements calming under his guidance.

The orb pulsed once, a wave of energy rippling outward. The cavern trembled, and for a moment, Aryan felt the weight of the Loom itself pressing down on him.

As the light faded, the threads settled into a delicate weave. The air grew still, and Aryan let out a breath he hadn't realized he'd been holding.

But as he turned to leave, the Keeper's voice echoed once more. "You've chosen your path, Aryan. But beware—the Loom is watching, and its whispers grow louder."

***

# 29

# The Unseen Hand

The first signs of dawn broke over the horizon, casting a pale light on the uneven terrain Aryan now navigated. The artifact in his hand had grown warm, its glow steady but subdued, as though it shared in his uncertainty. The Keeper's words echoed in his mind, a shadow trailing him with each step.

He had mended the threads in the cavern, but their fragile balance lingered in his thoughts. The Loom, watching, whispering—what did it mean? Could the Veil's whispers be trusted, or was he weaving a pattern he didn't fully understand?

The path led Aryan into a dense forest, its canopy thick enough to obscure the rising sun. The air was alive with the rustle of leaves and distant bird calls, but an undercurrent of tension hummed just beneath.

As he ventured deeper, he noticed faint markings on the trees—symbols carved into the bark, their meaning elusive yet oddly familiar. They reminded him of the patterns in the threads he had seen, a language of the Loom etched into the world itself.

A sudden crack of a branch startled him. Aryan spun around, his senses sharp, but he saw no one. The forest seemed to hold its breath, the silence unnerving.

"Following me won't make you invisible," Aryan said, his voice cutting through the stillness.

From behind a cluster of trees, a figure emerged—a young woman, her hair tied back and her eyes sharp with suspicion. She held a simple dagger, its blade glinting faintly in the dim light.

"You're a hard one to track," she said, stepping closer but keeping her weapon at the ready.

Aryan raised an eyebrow. "And you are?"

"Rhea," she replied curtly. "And you've been tampering with things you shouldn't."

Aryan frowned. "If you're here to lecture me about the Loom, you're late. The Keeper already had their say."

Rhea tilted her head, her expression unreadable. "The Keeper isn't the only one watching. Every move you make ripples outwards, and not everyone agrees with how you're handling the threads."

Her words struck a chord, but Aryan kept his composure. "If you think you can do better, the Loom is all yours."

Rhea's gaze hardened. "This isn't about who's better. It's about the cost of what you're doing. Do you even understand the price you're paying?"

Aryan hesitated, the weight of her question pressing down on him. "What price? What are you talking about?"

Rhea stepped closer, lowering her dagger slightly. "The threads you mend—they don't just fix themselves. The Loom takes something in return. Energy, memories, life itself. You've been giving parts of yourself away with every weave, and you don't even realize it."

Aryan's heart skipped a beat. He thought back to the exhaustion that followed each mending, the strange gaps in his recollections. Had he been sacrificing pieces of himself without knowing?

"You're lying," Aryan said, though his voice wavered.

Rhea shook her head. "You think the Loom operates without balance? Every thread you touch shifts the weave, and the Loom demands payment for that shift. You've felt it, haven't you? The weariness, the fading edges of your memories?"

Aryan's grip on the artifact tightened. "If that's true, why didn't anyone tell me? Not the Keeper, not Kabir—no one."

"Because they wanted to see what you'd do," Rhea replied. "The Loom isn't just a tool, Aryan. It's alive, and it's testing you."

Aryan's mind raced, the implications unravelling before him. Was he truly saving the Loom, or was he being used as a pawn in a larger game? The thought chilled him, but another question burned in his mind.

"If the Loom takes something in return, then what about you?" he asked. "What price have you paid?"

Rhea's expression darkened, and for a moment, she seemed lost in thought. "Enough to know the cost isn't worth it," she said finally. "That's why I'm here—to stop you before you give too much."

Aryan took a step back, his instincts flaring. "Stop me? How?"

Rhea's grip on the dagger tightened. "By taking the artifact. It's the source of your connection to the Loom. Without it, you can't mend the threads, and the Loom can't take from you."

Aryan's eyes narrowed. "You think I'm just going to hand it over?"

"I was hoping you'd see reason," Rhea said, her voice edged with regret. "But if not, then I'll do what I have to."

The tension between them crackled like static, each moment stretching unbearably. Aryan's mind raced, weighing his options. The artifact pulsed in his hand, as though urging him to act.

"You don't understand," Aryan said, his voice firm. "I can't stop now. The Loom—whatever it's doing, whatever it's taking— needs to be preserved. If I walk away, everything unravels."

"And if you don't walk away?" Rhea countered. "What happens when there's nothing left of you to give?"

Aryan didn't answer. Instead, he turned and ran, the forest blurring around him as he pushed forward. He didn't know where he was going, only that he had to keep moving. Behind him, Rhea's voice rang out, sharp and determined. "You can't outrun the Loom, Aryan. And you can't outrun yourself."

***

# 30

# The Loom's Veil

The air shimmered as Aryan stepped into the heart of the Loom's sanctum—a cavernous expanse where light wove itself into intricate patterns. The threads pulsed with life, each one humming with a frequency that resonated in Aryan's chest. This was the core of it all, the source of the whispers, the burdens, and the choices that had brought him here.

Behind him, Kabir and Rhea stood at an uneasy distance, their silent tension as loud as the threads themselves. The artifact in Aryan's hand glowed brighter with each step he took, as though eager to reunite with the Loom.

"Is this what you wanted, Kabir?" Aryan asked, his voice steady despite the chaos brewing inside him. "To bring me here and let the Loom decide my fate?"

Kabir's expression was unreadable, his usual calm laced with something sharper. "It was never about what I wanted," he replied. "The Loom has always been the one calling to you. I only helped you hear its voice."

Aryan turned to Rhea; her dagger still sheathed but her stance guarded. "And you? What do you want?"

"I want to stop this," she said. "Whatever the Loom promises, it takes more than it gives. You've already paid too much, Aryan. Walk away before it's too late."

Aryan's grip tightened on the artifact. "Walk away? After everything? The threads are breaking, Rhea. If I leave now, there'll be nothing left."

The Loom pulsed, its glow intensifying. Aryan felt it tug at him, a silent plea that was impossible to ignore. He stepped closer, the threads seeming to ripple in response.

As he approached the Loom, a figure began to take shape in its light—a spectral form with features that mirrored Aryan's own, yet older, wearier.

"Who are you?" Aryan whispered.

The figure's voice was soft but firm, echoing with an otherworldly resonance. "I am the weaver who came before you. And the one who came before me. We are all threads in the same tapestry, Aryan. And now, you must choose whether to bind yourself to it—or let it unravel."

The figure stepped closer, and Aryan felt a wave of emotions wash over him: sorrow, hope, and a deep, aching loneliness. "You've seen the cost of weaving, haven't you? The memories, the energy, the very essence of who you are. The Loom does not take—it transforms. Every thread you mend becomes a part of you, and you a part of it."

Aryan's breath caught. The sacrifices he had made weren't simply lost—they had become woven into the fabric of the Loom itself.

"And if I stop?" Aryan asked, his voice barely audible.

The figure's expression softened. "Then the threads will fray, and the tapestry will fall apart. But you will remain whole, free to live your life unbound by its weight."

Kabir stepped forward, his voice breaking the silence. "Aryan, listen to me. This isn't just about you. The Loom holds the balance of countless lives, countless worlds. If it falls, so does everything connected to it."

Rhea's voice cut through like a blade. "And what about him, Kabir? What about Aryan? How much more of himself does he have to give before there's nothing left?"

The tension between them hung heavy in the air, but Aryan barely heard them. His gaze was fixed on the Loom, its light pulsating with an urgency that mirrored the beating of his heart.

With a deep breath, Aryan stepped forward, the artifact in his hand glowing brighter than ever. The Loom's threads seemed to reach for him, their light wrapping around his form.

For a moment, time seemed to stand still. Aryan saw flashes of everything he had sacrificed—the memories of his father, the quiet moments of peace, the parts of himself he could no longer name.

But he also saw what he had preserved: the lives saved, the worlds kept whole, the balance maintained.

And then, he made his choice.

***

# 31

# The Final Thread

The Loom's light engulfed Aryan, its warmth both comforting and overwhelming. As he reached out, the threads seemed to hum in recognition, their patterns shifting and realigning.

The artifact in his hand dissolved, its energy merging with the Loom. Aryan felt a surge of power unlike anything he had ever known, followed by a profound stillness.

When the light faded, Aryan stood alone. The Loom was quiet, its threads steady and unbroken. But something had changed.

Kabir and Rhea approached cautiously, their expressions a mix of relief and apprehension.

"Aryan?" Kabir asked, his voice tentative.

Aryan turned to face them, his eyes glowing faintly with the light of the Loom. "It's done," he said simply.

Rhea's gaze searched his face. "And you? What did it take from you?"

Aryan hesitated, then smiled—a sad, weary smile. "Enough. But not everything."

As they stepped out of the sanctum, the world seemed different. The air was lighter, the colours more vivid. The Veil was still there, but its whispers were softer, more distant.

Aryan knew his journey wasn't over. The Loom had given him a new purpose, one he didn't fully understand yet. But for the first time, he felt at peace with the uncertainty.

**Epilogue: The Quiet Thread**

Years later, in a quiet village at the edge of the world, a child sat by a fire, listening to a story told by an old man with kind eyes. The story was about a weaver who had saved the world by sacrificing a part of himself.

As the firelight flickered, the child asked, "What happened to the weaver? Did he live happily ever after?"

The old man smiled, his gaze distant. "He lived," he said. "And sometimes, that's enough."

The child nodded, satisfied, and the old man leaned back, watching the flames dance. Somewhere, in the quiet of the night, the Loom hummed softly, its threads unbroken.

***

www.ingramcontent.com/pod-product-compliance
Lightning Source LLC
Chambersburg PA
CBHW021547150726
47990CB00006B/2428